A LABORING HAND

REFLECTIONS: BOOK 2

SHARON HUGHSON

First Edition © January 14, 2020

©Sharon L. Hughson

Published by InkSpired in Portland, Oregon

Cover Art by Rachel543 on Fiverr

Editing by Kristen Corrects, Inc.

For all the Marthas in the world who worship through their work

PREFACE

Behind the Story

While I was diligently writing two Christian romance novellas in November 2018, this story kept rearing its head. Eventually, I gave in and wrote a couple of scenes. That's the moment the Lord impressed on me that the focus for my writing was going to undergo a metamorphosis. Rather than writing mostly romance with an occasional Bible study, He wanted me to spend the next year writing a series about real women who walked beside Jesus Christ in first-century Israel.

Wow. I hardly read historical fiction. I couldn't possibly write it. Or so I told myself.

His answer to my doubts? *I can do all things through Christ* (Philippians 4:13), and faithful is the God who called me to write, who will also do the writing (I Thessalonians 5:24).

And while I was writing the next two stories, Martha and her sister taught me an important truth we all need to grasp if we are to boldly serve the Lord:

Work Can Be Worship

I hope you will see this and many more truths as you read Martha's story.

My Purpose in Writing This

My first purpose is to obey God.

But I need you to understand *Reflections: A Laboring Hand* is a fictionalization. This means the story is based on some actual events (and the scripture references for these will be included in every chapter when they exist), but it isn't meant to be received as if it were a true story. I have crafted a storyline with drama and tension for Martha that expands on the facts given in the Bible. I tried to keep my suppositions about Martha's family life realistic to the times. This required a boatload of research.

The major sources for information I used as a supplement my imagination: The Holy Bible KJV, Judaism 101 (at jewfaq.org), HolyLandNetwork.com, BiblicalChronology.com, Bible History Online, CookingwiththeBible.com, and Biblehub.com. Yes, I even searched images through Wikipedia.

I'm an author, not a Bible scholar nor a historian. I believe the scriptures are God-breathed and essential for successful living. I'm just a lay-woman trying to live for Christ in the twenty-first century.

I wrote this novella to encourage women to live for the Lord. God has called me to write stories that meet others where they are and offer hope for the path ahead. I pray this story does that for everyone who reads it.

God gave us the Bible to guide our lives. To truly understand God's Word, we need to understand its context. The people whose lives scripture recorded are humans, with flaws, faults, and failures much like our own. Once we grasp this reality, we can serve our Lord with confidence and freedom.

I've been enamored of Martha of Bethany for many years, and I recently determined that she's gotten a bad rap in too many sermons. During my research phase, I also read some current nonfiction Christian living books that used Martha as an example. One book I recommend if you want to study more about Martha is *Made Like Martha* by Katie M. Reid. This book is written in a relatable style that immediately engaged me.

What this Story Isn't

This fictionalized story is not intended to make any doctrinal statements or defend any specific stances. Neither is it an endorsement of any facts outside those found in the Holy Bible, King James Version, which is quoted and footnoted within.

This story isn't meant to glorify Martha of Bethany, either. Martha was a friend of our Lord Jesus Christ while he lived as a man. She is an example for women of all eras who want to befriend Jesus Christ, and she is often vilified as a non-example.

One beta reader told me she'd read Martha was a wealthy woman, and she had a hard time relating to my story because it portrays Martha differently. If you have read other stories about Martha of Bethany, I hope they helped you understand her willingness to serve. In my research of Martha, I found mostly "traditions," and nothing really clicked with me. It did not make sense to me that a wealthy woman would be so focused on working, working, working and serving, serving, serving. Maybe because I'm not wealthy, I found I could relate better to a poor woman who struggled each day. In truth, the Martha you'll meet in these pages is neither poor nor rich (but be aware there was no middle class in the Roman Empire, so she lives more like a plebian than a patrician). She has plenty to eat and a comfortable home, but she is not living in the same "station" as she had before her parents died.

The Martha I found while studying scripture and outside sources in preparation for telling her "story" was a Type-A perfectionist who embraced her responsibility to family with seriousness and dedication. As a Type-A perfectionist raised by a Type-A perfectionist, I found plenty of things to relate to in Martha's heart. My prayer is that you will also find something of yourself in Martha as you read this fictional recounting of her relationship with her siblings and her Lord.

The *Reflections* Series

This is the second book in a planned series of three biblical retellings. These stories are based on the changed hearts and lives of real women who lived and walked with Jesus Christ over twenty centuries ago. I can hardly fathom the scope of it.

In truth, I can only imagine life in first-century Israel, but since imagination is part of my gifting from God, what better way to use it than bringing the scriptures to life for others? Based on reviews from readers of *A Pondering Heart* (the first in the *Reflections* series), it's finding its mark.

Vicki from Wyoming says: "There are no words to sufficiently describe this BEAUTIFUL story. As a mother and a lover of my Lord – this book moved and touched me deeply."

Jessica says: "This book takes a brave look at Mary's life and shows the human side to her, bringing the reader into her world and her mind. I wish this was required reading for CCD classes! Not only was I drawn into Mary's story, her fears, her hopes, her dreams, I was amazed at the historical detail and the biblical accuracy as well. Highly recommended!"

My Invitation

Welcome to my word-powered time machine. Step inside the portal of imagination as I set the dials to the calendar year

23 AD. The location arrow points directly to an insignificant village within the vast Roman Empire: a place called Bethany, in the land of Israel in the region of Judea.

Close the hatch on your present-day world, and enter the Palestine of our Lord and Savior, Jesus Christ.

MY TWENTY-THIRD SUMMER

*D*ust puffed around my sandals, and I pressed my shawl closer to my mouth. Even with the sun hovering close to the horizon, summer beat against my shoulders, making my tunic stick to my back. My neighborhood's single-level homes offered nothing to shade me from the day's heat.

My lower back and shoulders throbbed. Today was the day I cleaned for the only Pharisee on my short list of customers. Bethany's proximity to Jerusalem invited the presence of important people, but I hadn't been hired by them.

Thank you, Yahweh.

Simon's demands couldn't curdle goat's milk, but his wife was a worse tyrant than Herod the Great. And the older folks still talked about when he went crazy and slew hundreds of baby boys.

Finally, I rounded the final corner and dropped my hand

from my lips. The simple house where I grew up stood at the end of the short street.

Home.

Smoke curled from coals in the fire pit a few steps from the front door where a sheepskin, nailed out of the way to allow a non-existent breeze to cool the interior, offered warmth and privacy in the evening. The familiar sight calmed me. Various jugs lined the exterior wall, shaded from the sun by the wooden eaves Abba had nailed in place so long ago. I could almost see Mother stringing up wet clothes under those eaves and picture Grandmother stretching a freshly woven rug.

I blinked. Nothing hung there now. The looms had been sold after my father passed away eight years ago. Men from the Weavers' Guild wouldn't allow me to be a member, and the only male left in our home had been ten at the time.

We'd learned to live without the looms and the guild. The plague had killed my mother and older brother, but what it had stolen was harder to accept. The loss had broken my father's heart, and the disease left my only brother an invalid. I shook the thoughts away.

I miss you, Abba.

I gritted my teeth to keep the emotion from weakening my weary spirit. There were duties to perform. I hoped Taz had opened the shutters on the window in his room. Surely, he'd remembered to do something so ordinary before diving into his latest obsession.

At the sill of the door, I slid my sandals off. My feet weren't much cleaner than the leather, but the packed dirt floor didn't stir under bare feet the way it would beneath sandals. Or so Grandmother always said. I missed her and her wisdom, too.

I stepped into our expansive main room, easily as large as most of the houses on our street. When Abba and Mother lived, they worked their looms close to the doorway in summer and toward the fireplace on the right-hand wall during winter months.

Now, the long table centered in the room and worn cushions around it were the only furnishings that remained—except for the small loom leaning against the wall shared with the room where my sister and I slept. The scent of ink warred with the lingering woodsmoke, and I swallowed a frustrated huff.

Lazarus lounged near the table, his shriveled right arm resting on a smaller pillow at his side, a scroll unrolled before him. I hoped it was the account list he kept for my cleaning and catering clients. Although his body wasn't whole, he was better at sums and keeping a ledger than I was.

But lately, he'd been distracted from the work I needed him to do. He'd been begging the three local scribes for copies of Isaiah's prophetic accounts. All because of the crazy speculation that John bar Zebedee was a prophet and some cousin of his was a miracle worker.

Eyes the same dark brown as mine glanced up from the parchment. "You look tired."

I was always tired.

I studied the scruffy beard that tried to cover his weak chin. Although I was six years older than Laz, we carried similar features, like the broad forehead and nose of our father. Even if he had been whole, my brother wasn't a handsome man any more than I was a comely woman.

Probably why you're unmarried. The voice in my head sounded like my grandmother, but she'd never said anything so cruel while she lived. Although if she'd known I'd let her die for a few extra minutes of sleep, perhaps she would have.

I buried the old nightmares and shuffled on aching feet toward the preparation counter along the far wall. I needed to prepare our meal.

"Mary?" I glanced toward our shared room. The flax curtain we used for privacy was pinned aside, as was the one shielding what had once been our parents' room. The open curtain meant Mary wasn't there.

I sighed and trudged toward the slab of wood that served as our counter. Flour and oil containers sat alongside the simple pottery bowls we used to prepare and eat our meals.

"Haven't seen her. Probably still at Avi's."

Avi. The kindness in his midnight-sky eyes and full-lipped smile flashed into my mind. I shoved the vision away. The old man had a wife. Plus, he was a client I couldn't afford to lose, and I wouldn't risk Mary's place as weaving instructor to his three daughters for anything. As long as she worked, the pressure Laz and I faced to accept one of the marriage suitors didn't overwhelm us.

But she should marry. Mary will have a family one day.

I shed my shawl, draping it on the cushion across the table from my brother. As much as I despised the clutter, I'd be forced to don it again if I needed to barter for more supplies. Why hadn't I stopped at the market on my way home? Right. The thought of dealing with another demanding person shriveled my insides like a grape left too long on the vine.

I reached for the bread ingredients. My hands were red from the harsh cleaner I'd used earlier. I stared at my fingers, reminded of my grandmother's hands. Yes, I was an old maid of twenty-three winters, but my hands looked as rough as hers, and she lived to sixty-six summers.

I removed the lid from the flour. There wasn't as much in the pot as when I'd baked bread yesterday.

"Did you make bread today?"

I turned to see the blank expression on my brother's face. He'd started to return his attention to the scrolls, and I noticed they were covered in faded scrawls. Not the accounts then.

Heat flooded my cheeks. I whirled back to the cooking, hiding my irritation from him. Couldn't I count on Laz to keep track of the accounts before chasing some wild notion?

"Maybe she's baking it now." I muttered the words mostly to myself.

But my comment made no logical sense. Why wasn't Mary using the stone in our outside pit? If she chose to wait in line at the communal oven, it probably meant she was listening for the gossip that fueled our brother's daydreams of Messiah.

Worry warred with irritation. She shouldn't run about town alone.

My fingers groped for the jar of lentils on the supply shelf overhead. I'd start the soup and hope she showed up before I made a batch of bread we didn't need, since keeping it fresh was no easy feat.

"Will you build up the fire?" I stared at my brother.

His eyes had a glazed look, and I hoped it wasn't another fever. No matter what I did to protect him, it seemed he was sick every winter. The physician told me that his body would have a hard time fighting disease since the poliomyelitis had decimated his insides along with shrinking his left leg and withering his right arm.

"Lazarus." I raised my voice, hands paused in the reach for the knife used to chop vegetables.

He nodded and pushed to his feet. His limp seemed more pronounced as he headed outside, and my father's old robe hung on his frame. I remembered when Mother made it for Abba. The evenly striped pattern of her weave had been oft requested by the customers.

While my hands chopped ingredients and added them to the pot, my mind danced around numerous worries. How would we pay a physician if Lazarus got sick again? Where was Mary? Should we agree to the latest offer for her hand? Why had my father given up on life? I needed him to take charge of these difficult negotiations.

If he was still alive, maybe I would have a husband and home of my own.

I gritted my teeth over the useless thoughts. I knew I should pray instead of worry. Grandmother had told me to do that more times than I could recollect. But prayer involved deeper thought. After yet another grueling day as the head of the household, I didn't have the mind for it.

The unacknowledged head, a discontent voice whispered.

Laz returned and rolled up the scroll. He was halfway to his room, and I was lifting the pot of soup when Mary burst into the house.

"It's true!" She was breathless, and her cheeks were flushed. I shouldn't have been able to see them, but her veil was askew, hanging down her back with her long, thick braid.

Her eyes, more amber than mine, glowed with excitement. Her comely face, nearly a replica of our mother's, creased with a smile.

My heart lurched. My sister was a flower among thorns in Bethany, and I couldn't let my desire for her to find a perfect spouse lead her into spinsterhood. Our cousin Nathan had offered to find a contractual arrangement for her, but I couldn't trust him to protect her heart above financial considerations.

I marveled over her joyful entrance even as I wondered, *When was the last time I truly smiled?*

I worked hard six days each week. I provided sustenance for my siblings, and I worried about how to best guide them. That didn't leave much time for joy.

What did I have to be joyful about? What did she?

Lazarus turned to her. "Where?"

I blinked at him. Obviously, they carried on a conversation, and I wasn't a part of it. Suddenly, I felt old enough to be their mother. Once we were siblings who shared everything, even if I was nearly ten years older than our baby sister.

"At the temple. But the rumor is he'll be returning to Galilee after the Sabbath."

The Sabbath was the day after tomorrow. Maybe I should have prepared the extra bread.

Laz clutched the scroll closer. "We must travel there tomorrow. Stay with cousin Nathan."

Mary nodded.

"What are you two plotting? And you know better than to invite yourself to Nathan's house." The man had never forgiven them for surviving the plague that killed his siblings and parents.

"Avi's family has a house near the temple." Mary sidled closer, and the scent of fresh bread crowded out the hint of remaining leeks from my soup preparations. "We can sleep on their roof."

I shook my head and finally noticed the cloth-wrapped package in her hands.

"I made extra bread for the journey and the Sabbath." She placed it on the wooden plank beside the remnants of the spices I'd chopped for the soup.

"Thank you. Put this on the fire." I handed her the pot, and she hurried outside, eager as always to please and obey. Why hadn't I gotten even a drop of that tender spirit?

It wouldn't have survived the loss of your family and dreams.

I glared at Laz. "What are you talking about?"

"Yeshua of Nazareth. He's teaching in the temple."

Not Yeshua of Nazareth again. If only my brother could work a trade, he wouldn't have time to sit around dreaming about Messiah and imagining that Yeshua was the Anointed One.

"Mary has responsibilities here." I wanted to tell him he couldn't go. That travel always taxed him, and I feared he'd get sick again.

But he was the oldest male and, according to the law, the head of this household. No one cared that I worked day and night and bore every emotional burden. Maybe my mother had, too. Perhaps that was a woman's lot in life, but I had no one to ask.

He raised his chin, and I was reminded of Abba. "We'll leave after she finishes with her lessons. Avi has promised the use of his cart whenever we travel to the city."

Avi's kindness knew no boundaries toward this house full of orphans. But I wouldn't allow my family to become indebted to him.

More indebted.

"Avi is kind, but we shouldn't take advantage of him."

"He offered." Lazarus shuffled closer. His hand felt slightly feverish on mine, and a rock dropped in my empty stomach. "You must come with us. Once you hear Yeshua of Nazareth, you'll see I'm right."

I wanted to shake him off. The list of responsibilities to be seen to grew day by day and making an extra trip to Jerusalem didn't fit into my busy schedule. I'd rather work at the loom on the Sabbath, not fret about traveling home before the sun set.

Mary skipped back inside. I gave her feet a pointed look. She backtracked to the door to leave her sandals beside mine.

"I can't wait to hear Yeshua teach. Do you think he'll heal anyone?" Her mouth widened into a pert circle. "Maybe he'd heal your arm."

Laz shook his head. "I don't want anything from him. Only to learn if he is the Anointed One. If he is, then I'll follow him."

It was the most absurd thing he'd said yet. "You'll do no such thing," I said. "You can barely walk to the community oven. You aren't following this stranger all over the countryside."

Laz stared at me, unblinking. "Where is your faith, sister?"

The question burned through my chest and scalded something deep in my heart. Even now, replaying the events so I can write them here, the words bury a spike in my uneasy conscience.

Did I lose my faith when my mother and brother died? Or did it happen the morning I ignored my grandmother's cry for my help?

Or had the final death knell rung when I became the head of this family? I carried every burden to keep my siblings from those worries.

Where was my faith? Buried with my parents.

MY TWENTY-THIRD SUMMER

The cart's wheel squawked as we topped the rise to the city gate. Jerusalem, finally. Our journey was half-finished now, and I sighed, taking a swipe at the sweat trapped against my scalp. At least traveling to the guild quarter and cousin Nathan's residence was easier, thanks to the cobbled Roman road.

The traffic doubled on the capital's streets. Avi's donkey plodded forward, flicking an ear when a team of oxen pulling a loaded wagon in the opposite direction bellowed. The fetid city scents made my stomach churn. I pressed my shawl over my nose and mouth, but I still tasted the foulness of waste and overcrowding.

Mary walked briskly beside the donkey, scanning the streets. Somehow, she managed to keep her head bowed slightly. Laz didn't hide his interest in the shops and people we passed.

Multiple turns later, we entered a narrow street that led to the back gates to various guild member homes lining Weaver Street. Most of these had shops on the main street, but our cousin no longer had the manpower to run a shop. His neighbor, a tentmaker, had taken over that space and allowed Nathan's rugs to hang on the walls. Nathan sold wares that way and gained orders, but he treated it like a shameful secret.

The house was large and formal compared to our place, but it wasn't fancy like Simon's home. *Simeon the Master Weaver*, the sign beside the door announced. That was my uncle, and he'd never fully recovered from the poliomyelitis that took the rest of our family. When he died less than a year later, Nathan became an orphan.

I helped Laz from the cart. Mary knocked on the back gate. The serving boy, Liakim, answered. His mother had been part of the household since before he was born. At ten, he was nearly as tall as Mary.

"Mary!" He adored her. "Master Nathan isn't expecting you." His smile faded.

I despised that the boy called Nathan "Master." If it wasn't for Liakim's mother, Nathan would have lost everything. When the rest of his family lay ill with fever, Sarah stayed and cared for them. She deserved to be honored as a family member, but my opinion on the matter wasn't welcomed in this house.

"We've come to hear Yeshua of Nazareth."

"The healer?" At Mary's nod, Liakim's gaze strayed to

Laz. Like everyone else—including Yeshua of Nazareth, I was certain—the boy assumed my brother wanted to be healed.

But I knew he didn't. His mission and desire was to determine if this stranger from Galilee was Messiah. I could tell him, but I'd permit him find out on his own. Abba said things we learned that way wouldn't ever leave us.

Just so this obsession ends.

We followed Liakim to his mother's side. The boy hurried back to care for the animal and cart while Sarah led us into the main room. Nathan sat behind a loom. The gentle twanging of the threads as he quickly laced wool through them was a melody from my childhood.

Yearning tugged my heart. I heard an echo of my father's booming voice and my mother's tinkling laughter. Once we were a happy family. I hardened myself against the wave of nostalgia. That was the past. The best I could hope for now was to make certain Mary had a happy and whole family for her future.

Sarah said, "Your cousins from Bethany, Master."

I stiffened and advanced into the room.

Nathan's hand stilled, and he looked up slowly. His hazel eyes—a greenish-golden-brown nothing like ours or his father's—narrowed.

"Cousins. I wasn't expecting company." He said it with a cutting tone that made his displeasure evident.

I hated playing this game. His words said *family*, but their delivery said *you're bothering me*, and my spirit railed. I bit back a rude retort that would have reminded him of Grandmother's tongue lashing if he'd ever been less than welcoming to family in her presence.

"Lazarus and Mary are on a mission to hear the Galilean speak."

His thick brows rose toward his thinning hairline. "Following the rumors of healing, are you?" His lip curled as he glanced at Lazarus. It made his plain face even less attractive.

My brother bowed his head slightly. "No, but I have my reasons."

Why didn't he spout his declaration that Yeshua was Messiah? I advanced toward my cousin, who sighed and slipped from behind the loom. Our cheeks brushed together. I puckered my lips to give the kiss of greeting, but Nathan pulled away before I could deposit it on the side of his face. A hint of mint rose from him, and his beard scratched my jaw.

Once he'd given the same rushed greeting to my brother and sister, he settled at the loom. "Sarah can get you some refreshment."

I raised my eyebrows at Mary. "Mary will bring it."

Her shoulders sagged, but she followed the servant from the room. I despised being waited on, especially in this house where Sarah was more of a dear family member than the man who shared my blood.

Conversation waned to nothing as Nathan returned to work. Mary brought a tray and offered refreshments, but a few minutes after I drained the cup of watered wine[1], I excused myself.

Tomorrow would be a long day and accompanying me to our chamber helped Mary escape Nathan, who hadn't missed a beat before asking her to create "one of those rugs she designs so well." As if we owed him for the hospitality.

Grandmother would have had plenty to say about that.

CROWDS FUNNELED ALONG THE STREET, but no vendors clogged the way. Today, worshipers on their way to or from the temple made up the press. Lazarus tugged my arm. His breath came in short gasps, and I tried to slow him with a pull of my own, but I'd never seen him so focused and eager.

I heard the voice before we entered the outer court of worship. Masculine and level, it carried over the mass of shuffling feet and bleating animals. How was such a thing possible?

When I saw the man sitting on an overturned cart, I stopped. Laz pushed ahead, weaving his way through the press of listeners, and Mary bumped into me. Her breath warmed my shoulder as she peered through the assembled bodies.

Yeshua's brown eyes were flecked with amber, and his face was broad, unremarkable under the shoulder-length hair and scruffy beard. There were no obvious evidences of piety —no frontlets like a priest might wear, *payot* the Pharisees favored, or prayer shawl like a rabbi carried—but something in his voice resonated inside me.

He told a story of a man finding a pearl of great price in a field and bankrupting himself to purchase the property. My ears tuned into the tale. It had been years since a man's story-telling had interested me. My heart yearned for Abba. Would it ever stop?

As I listened, I sensed a deeper meaning to this man's tale. A frisson of flutters moved in my chest, like I used to experience when the rabbi read the scrolls. Before my life changed. Before everything was stolen from me.

His story ended, and the hypnotic effect of his voice with it. Someone standing close to him asked a question I didn't hear.

Mary pressed her mouth to my ear. "Let's get closer. With Laz."

I allowed her to guide me through the crowd. Some people pushed toward us, going in the opposite direction, their temple business done. They had no interest in Yeshua of Nazareth. Others pressed closer. I saw a man who trembled from some disease held upright by two younger men, trying to get close enough for healing.

Laz had molded himself to the edge of a group of scribes. One of them asked a question about the law as Mary pressed beside our brother, whispering something in his ear. He shook his head. What were they talking about now? Was she asking if he would be healed? I couldn't imagine what our life might be like if Laz worked and took his place as the head of our house.

As Yeshua answered the scribe with another story, something hard inside my chest began softening. This was how I had often felt during my childhood as I listened to the weavers discuss scripture. Often, they sang as they worked, but at the beginning of each week, they discussed the reading from the synagogue. Their faith was simple but true. I hadn't always understood what they said, but I knew they believed in the Creator, the One True G-d of Abraham.

How had I let that slip away?

A hot tear spilled from my eye. As I reached to press my veil into it, Yeshua's dark gaze froze me. Rather than the impatience or patronization I often sensed from the rabbis and priests, I read only understanding in those deep pools.

You are seen. You are cared for. A long-silent voice spoke the affirmations to my spirit.

The moment of connection lasted long enough for me to choke back a sob. I was a sinner, and I had shown only outward contrition for many years. If I wanted to be right with Yahweh, I needed to confess.

Who is Yeshua to make me feel such things? I believe Messiah will come but is this man The One?

That evening during the temple sacrifice as the priest beseeched G-d for all of us, hands extended toward Heaven, I voiced my own petition to the G-d of my father.

I'm sorry, Yahweh. I've been a terrible daughter to You. I am not the mother of Lazarus and Mary, but they have You as their Father. Thank You for Yeshua of Nazareth. I see You in his eyes. Help me learn from his teachings.

For the first time, I considered that Lazarus might be right about the teacher who worked miracles. Was Yeshua of Nazareth Israel's Messiah?

MY TWENTY-THIRD AUTUMN

A month had passed since I came face-to-face with my sinfulness in the eyes of a simple carpenter. Yeshua had graciously attended a meal in our home, and I was almost glad that Laz took to his bed for a week after the Sabbath in Jerusalem. Illness kept him from running after Yeshua of Nazareth.

I kept working but worried less because I'd begun praying more. It shocked me how much it soothed the rough places inside me. Was there really so much power in these simple petitions to G-d?

Today, there was too much for me to think about to wonder if Laz would run after Yeshua's crowd of disciples the next time they met. On top of my regular cooking, cleaning, and caretaking jobs, things had taken a sad turn at Avi's home.

This was the time of year he served his priestly courses at

the temple, and his wife Jochebed suffered from an increasing fever. A couple of years ago, she'd lost her son during child-birth, and since that time she'd had a weak constitution. Like every Jewish woman, she wanted to give her husband an heir.

Avi had lost so much already. After the same epidemic that decimated my family and much of Bethany, his first wife had perished in a different plague. Within a year, he'd married young Jochebed.

Yahweh, ease her pain. Bring peace to the home.

The prayer squelched the bitter memories of my own losses and constant guilt for surviving. I concentrated on the open flame in the kitchen courtyard. I boiled the sheets, praying that the sickness would be cleansed from them. I was blessed to work in the home of Avi the scribe, which was how he was known during the half-year he didn't serve in the temple.

Should I send a runner to the temple?

Unless I sent a message, Avi would stay in Jerusalem until the Sabbath. Would Jochebed make it two more days?

Yahweh, please let this woman live to see her husband one more time.

Seven years ago, I had begun working in this home to care for Avi's mother and firstborn son. Jochebed had only been his bride for two years, and she took deathly ill during her first pregnancy. From the first, she seemed overwhelmed by the multitude of tasks expected of a mistress of a large house, and she often left Avi's son from his first wife in the care of the old woman.

During their marriage, Jochebed had given Avi a daughter, a son, two more daughters, and then the baby who passed away. She'd done her part as the wife of a priest who wanted to pass his heritage to a son. Sadly, two years after Avi's eldest son passed, the younger boy died of the wasting cough. Even though Jochebed faded more with every pregnancy, she seemed determined to fulfill her duty.

G-d had a different plan.

Would Avi grieve? Their marriage was amicable, but I rarely saw the pair together except when their daughters were in attendance. I never saw them exchange the small looks my parents had shared, and these days, my sister spent more time with the girls than either of their parents.

"Martha."

I started at the cook's voice. Although she wasn't yet forty summers old, the woman was as wrinkled as a raisin.

"Mistress Jochebed calls for you."

I nodded and wiped my hands and brow on the linen towel that hung beside the kitchen doorway. My sandals scraped on the cobbled hallway. Avi provided well for his family, and he'd been more than generous with my siblings and me. Charity for the orphans, like the law demanded. He was the type of man I would want to marry. If I still had a chance for that.

Stop whimpering. The command sounded in Grandmother's voice. She'd used the stern tone with Mary, too, but nothing kept my sister from her daydreams. I was glad one of us could escape the hardships of reality in some way.

Jochebed, who was only five years older than me, wasted

away in a sickbed. Her breathing was harsh. Her forehead was pale and clammy, and her gray-streaked braids hung listlessly over her frail shoulders.

"Send a message to the temple." Her voice faltered. "Write it for me."

I bustled around her bed to the small table, my heart nearly choking me. I offered her a small sip of the medicinal drink sitting there, and she could barely swallow. She waved it away. Next to a hairbrush sat a stash of square parchment, an inkwell and stylus, and a blotter.

I knelt and prepared the tip of the stylus.

"I'm ready."

"The end is near." She panted. The wheezing of her breaths sent chills up my spine. "Come quickly for the girls."

I scratched out the letters. I glanced up, but her eyes were closed.

"Will you sign it?"

Her chin trembled but lowered slightly, and her eyes fluttered open. After reinking the stylus, I took the wooden lid from the paper box and settled the parchment on it. Her hand shook as she scrawled the characters for her name at the bottom of the note.

"I will get the fastest runner." Several orphans who lived with the rabbi were always eager to earn an extra coin. They could be trusted to deliver the message.

"Thank you." Her eyes closed, and, although I stood at her bedside, her whispered words hardly reached my ear.

I rushed to blot the note and seal it with wax. Mary met me in the hallway, and I shook my head at her. In the afternoon, the girls would ask to see their mother if she was feeling up to visitors.

Later at the market, as I slid another bundle of herbs into the makeshift sling of my shawl, I wondered if Avi would make it home in time. Once Jochebed was gone, should I ask him to consider Mary for the position of governess? At thirteen, she was young for such a position of responsibility, but his daughters were younger and loved her.

Maybe he would consider Mary as his next wife?

I shook away the thought, ignoring the way my heart dove into my stomach. My family came from the tribe of Benjamin. He would have to give up his priestly duties if he married outside the tribe of Levi. Anyway, that's how I thought it worked. I didn't know the law as well as Laz, but if I asked him such a pointed question about priests, he would wonder if I wanted Avi for myself.

Don't you?

I turned my attention to the crowded streets to drown out the voice in my head. I pushed through the throngs at the market. A dog barked, and a herd of kids rushed through the press, tagged by a shepherd boy younger than Mary.

Guilt lanced me. *Not at the expense of dutiful Jochebed.* Besides, I was past the age when men would consider me as a virgin bride. This would be my twenty-fourth winter, and there were plenty of younger, prettier, unspoiled girls—like Mary—to keep men from giving me a second look.

Yahweh, ease Jochebed's agony. If it is her time, let it be swift and painless. If it is your will, raise her from this bed of sickness.

The supplication yanked my mind back to the right place.

A dark-skinned potter said, "Yeshua of Nazareth baptizes like John." This was old news, but the words pulled me further from my pointless ruminations.

"Yeshua of Nazareth returns from Galilee. He fed multitudes with a few loaves." This was spoken by a woman whose baby was tied to her back.

"Yeshua of Nazareth cast demons out of a crazy woman who'd been telling fortunes."

"Yeshua..."

Always, the carpenter-turned-miracle worker was at the center of village gossip. For me, the litany of his amazing acts continued at home. Laz had heard Yeshua would be present for Sukkot,[1] and he was going to join his band of followers.

I dragged my way home only to have my siblings filled with talk of Yeshua of Nazareth too. "Invite him here." I should have considered the invitation longer.

"Do you mean it?" Mary's eyes glowed.

"He doesn't travel alone." Laz sat up straighter. "A dozen men are always with him."

I sighed. "Do any of them limp along?"

Laz blinked at me. "I can walk as well as anyone."

"Until another fever strikes." I sidled behind him, putting a hand on his shoulder like Abba did when he was correcting our weaving. "Who will care for you then?"

My brother grunted.

"Can't you be his disciple in Bethany?" Mary's question sliced through the tension between us.

Laz furrowed his thin brows and touched his lip.

"You could meet with other believers here." There were many, I knew, but to entice my brother, it would need to be someone important. "Hasn't Simon been his disciple since he cured the leprosy?"

The thought of Simon's wife made my stomach knot. She'd railed on me to clean with even more vigor in those days. When his skin had shown the pasty sign of the skin disease, he hadn't separated himself. Curiously, certain laws didn't seem to apply to Pharisees. Although, his case of leprosy had been mild, easily covered by bandages.

Laz nodded slowly. "Perhaps. I will invite him here, Martha. But it will be extra work for all of us."

"I'll help." Mary scuttled closer, her lovely face alight with a smile.

"Avi may need you once Jochebed passes." My gut wrenched at the thought of his grief.

Mary nodded. "The girls are old enough to be more responsible. They just need someone to direct them." She grinned. "Maybe Avi will hire you for that position."

Heat seeped from my scalp and bled into my face. Was my interest in Avi obvious?

"He should take another wife." Laz gave me a meaningful stare.

My throat tried to close. I cleared it. "We'll be happy to welcome Yeshua and his disciples. Some have family in Jerusalem. Perhaps they will take the time to visit them."

"Should I suggest that when I extend the invitation?"

I frowned. "Hospitality is extended to all."

The joy beaming from my siblings could have lit the

room. My tired lips turned up. *It takes less energy to smile than to frown*, Grandmother always said.

It would be wonderful to hear Yeshua teach again. His stories always reminded me to redirect my thoughts to heavenly things.

What was a little extra cooking and cleaning? I was an expert at those things. It wouldn't be a hardship, especially since my siblings promised to help me.

MY TWENTY-THIRD WINTER

I scurried home from Avi's house, angry at myself for not accepting his invitation to host Yeshua and his disciples. The central courtyard of his home was three times the size of my entire house, and his kitchen was large enough to prepare the extra food.

But I'm the hostess.

Besides, this was nothing new. Yeshua's followers had been stopping by our home for months, ever since that first Sabbath in Jerusalem when Lazarus invited them to rest with us before beginning the trek back to Capernaum. A few of his followers seemed shocked by our modest home, but none of them complained about the simple fare or sleeping on the cushions and rugs in the central room. Yeshua refused Laz's offer of using his room each time.

"The Son of man has nowhere to lay his head, my friend," he said when my brother offered.

As I entered our yard, I nudged the heating flat stone in the fire pit with the toe of my sandal. Hot enough for bread. Good.

I rushed through the entrance, greeted by Mary singing sweetly in her gentle soprano voice. A dart pierced my heart. She looked and sounded like Mother, and when she turned to greet me, dark hair flowing over her shoulders, her hazel eyes glowed nearly as much as her face.

With every visit, she became more infatuated with Yeshua, and I needed to have a serious discussion with her about it so she would understand the reality. Laz told me that Yeshua's mission from G-d prohibited him from taking a wife.

Let this childish obsession pass.

I hated to see her broken-hearted. Life had been cruel enough to my youngest sibling; she didn't need love to add its own insult. Especially not since it was obvious Yeshua loved her. Yeshua loved all of us, and it shined from his amazing, compassionate eyes.

No time for this discussion today. Our guests would arrive soon.

"The beans?" I asked as I slipped my sandals off and moved them aside. Once Yeshua and his followers arrived, they would be a stumbling block.

She nodded, continuing her song rather than answering with words. The scent of bread wafted from the hearth where a pot bubbled over a low-burning flame.

"Has Laz gone for the wine?" I didn't have enough for twenty people to drink their fill, and I'd asked him to bargain for more. Because he was a man, the merchants in town bartered more fairly with him, and I was relieved to leave him with a list of what I needed and a coin purse.

Mary nodded again, ending her song on a high note.

"You worry too much."

"You don't worry enough," I countered. Those words would slap me in the face later, but when I snapped them at her, I believed them with all my heart.

Even though marriage proposals kept coming in, she still wasn't responsible enough to run a household.

Who are you to judge another?

I squelched the condemning voice. I had a duty to prepare Mary for being a wife because she would marry. I wanted her to love and respect her husband as much as Mother did Abba.

I'd accepted the truth that no man would love me the way Abba had loved Mother. I'd been around enough married couples to know it was a rare thing anyway. But I could help Mary find a suitable spouse, and Avi continued to help me by giving Mary more responsibilities with his daughters.

He's a good man. Thank you, Yahweh, for placing him in my life.

That was a prayer I'd prayed often in the past, and I felt certain I would voice it many more times. Avi the scribe was a man who loved G-d with all his might. That's the sort of man Mary should marry.

I washed my hands and began to chop the pungent herbs I would add to the beans. The pestle smashed the herbs with rhythmic efficiency. Mary pressed together flour, salt, and olive oil, intent on baking more bread.

"The stone was hot." The words had barely left my mouth when Laz limped in followed by a boy carrying a jug on his head.

"Leave it in the shade outside." I waved a hand to the boy. "We'll draw out into pitchers half-filled with water. That will make it last."

Laz nodded to the boy, gesturing to a place further along the house, away from the cooking fire and the chimney. I heard the jingle of coins.

"It's fresh but already watered," Laz said as he entered the house again.

"What proportion?" My brain estimated the amount of drink a dozen thirsty men would need.

"Thirty percent." Lazarus slouched against the wall. Weariness etched his features, but I knew he wouldn't rest. He was more eager for the visitors than any of us.

"We can safely add another twenty percent. Will you see to it?"

"I'll need to draw more water." Mary's hands hesitated over the dough. "They'll need what I drew for washing."

"They aren't Pharisees." I returned to my chopping. "They won't care about washing before they eat. Could you hand me the bowl of olives?" I gestured to the line of pottery on the shelf overhead.

Mary shoved Abba's weaving stool into place and stepped up to grasp the bowl. "I intend to wash their feet."

I froze. Why would she insist on doing that? It was a servant's job, and since we didn't have servants, none of our guests ever expected it.

"They'll just get dirty again when he leaves on Sunday."

"But they'll be clean for Sabbath."

Like that mattered in our small synagogue.

"There isn't enough water." That would solve it.

"I'll draw more."

"The bread needs baking. And the floor should be swept, and the cushions beaten. Plus, we'll need to get out all the extra rugs."

Lazarus sighed and pushed away from the wall. "I'll get started on the cushions."

I shook my head. With only one arm, it took him much longer to clean them. "I'll do it. Draw out the wine."

Laz blinked at me before sharing a look with Mary. It was an apologetic expression. He'd tried to aid her plan, but the bossy big sister nixed it. Something gnawed at my heart, but I ignored it. There was work to be done.

Soon enough, the laughter and banter of a crowd of dusty men filled the room. I welcomed them with a small bowl of water and a clean linen cloth. Well, it was clean for the first man or two who dried their hands.

Yeshua reclined at the head of the table on the largest cushion, one my parents had often shared. John bar Zebedee, one of the Boanerges, sat on it with the Master. He was only a couple years older than Mary and the youngest of all the Master's followers.

The crowd of dirty disciples flooded our home. Some chose to lean against the wall on rugs Laz had pulled from his room and ours. The dirt floor could hardly be seen with so many men sprawled on cushions and rugs.

Mary and I circulated with pitchers, filling every cup we owned, and still two men shared each one of the battered pottery pieces. Once we finished, I began to distribute bowls of spiced beans and cloth-wrapped packages of bread, still warm from their place on the hearth. I turned to ask Mary to assist me, but she'd seated herself cross-legged at Yeshua's feet, staring up as he started to teach.

I blinked hard. What on earth was she thinking? Was this her rebellion since I hadn't let her get water for foot washing? She was certainly positioned in a way that she could wash his feet if she had the supplies.

I continued bustling around taking care of our guests, but my frustration grew. Yeshua's authoritative voice, usually so soothing, fueled the ire inside me. He could make her help me. I glanced at Laz, but my brother was watching the Master and scribbling on a piece of parchment. Mary never once looked my way, even when I nudged her with my ankle as I passed to refill the cup John shared with Yeshua.

My siblings had promised to help when I'd mentioned inviting the group to stay over for more than a day. Now they sat there, enjoying Yeshua's teaching while I served everyone.

With a careful eye, I glanced at every cup and bowl. Levi raised his cup in my direction, and I sidled through the sprawled bodies to fill it, nearly tripping on another man's filthy feet.

The mud-caked toes never even flinched, and my bubble of anger swelled. I swallowed it and turned to top off his cup. He stared through me as if I were invisible but working in the

Pharisee's home had accustomed me to that. In the past, Yeshua's friends had been more gracious.

Unrest stirred inside me as I shuffled around, refilling cups and then fetching more bread to replenish the diminishing stacks. After refilling my pitcher from the jar stored beneath the eaves, I counted the loaves in the linen clothes on the counter. Only three dozen were left. Soon, I would need to bake more.

And that's when it became too much. I strode toward Yeshua holding the jug of watered wine aloft and jabbed my sister with a meaningful kick. She blinked, staring at me for a moment as if I'd woken her from a deep sleep.

As I filled the Lord's cup, I said, "Lord, don't you care that my sister has left me to serve alone[1]?"

A hush descended in the room. The wine trickled against what was in his cup. Our eyes met.

"Bid her to help me." Couldn't he see how much work needed to be done? And Mary was just sitting there like a useless lump.

"Martha." His voice was quieter than it had been, almost gentle.

At the sound of my name from his lips, the turmoil loosened inside me. Why had I waited so long to ask for his assistance? His dark eyes filled with understanding and concern. I knew he would help me because he cared about me.

"Martha, you're anxious and worried about many things[2]."

The comfort oozing through me turned sharp and

became a prickle of conviction. Worry was a sin. My father had told me so.

"But one thing is needful."

One thing? I wanted to jerk my hand around at the crowd of hungry men who needed food, drink, and places to sleep. There were many things that needed to be taken care of. I knew he could see that.

Yeshua sighed. His fingers rested on the handle of the pitcher beside mine. They were square and scuffed—working man's hands.

"And Mary hath chosen that good part." His voice rose slightly, but not with anger or impatience, and his hand dropped to his lap. "And that won't be taken away from her[3]."

Everything warred within me as I struggled to comprehend his words. Mary was sitting there while our guests needed food and drink. How was that better than helping me meet their needs?

With one long glance, he turned to scan the room. "A certain man..."

I recognized the beginning of a parable. Usually I loved his stories—they always carried so much spiritual significance. Tonight, I couldn't listen because the words he'd spoken to me stung my heart.

Mary hath chosen that good part.

I filled cups with lowered eyes. Tears burned at the back of my eyelids whenever I blinked, but I widened my eyes and jerked my shawl up to cover most of my face.

Mary sat at his feet doing nothing, but Yeshua said she'd chosen the good part. *Mary hath chosen that good part.* The words kept echoing all evening, drowning out the Master's stories and the disciples' questions.

Even now, as I'm writing about it, his gentle admonition stings somewhere deep in my soul. Was there something wrong with my desire to make the men comfortable? Did Yeshua not want a meal and refreshment while he was talking?

One thing is needful. What one thing?

Mary stirred on our shared bed. Her forehead wrinkled and then smoothed. As I'd helped her prepare for bed, I'd wanted to ask about the lessons, but I felt foolish. If I asked, she would know that I hadn't paid attention while Yeshua taught.

Why did that make me feel guilty? Yeshua wasn't angry with me. He even thanked me for the food and drink as I passed him to go to bed.

Yahweh help me understand what this means. What is the one needful thing for me to do? Sit and listen like my sister?

I sighed, and my heart weighed more heavily in my chest. *But if I do that, who will do the work?*

MY TWENTY-FOURTH WINTER

One thing is needful.

The words chased me through my days. Everywhere I went, they followed. Whether I was cleaning houses, caring for sick women, or serving at large feasts hosted by the wealthier citizens of Bethany, Yeshua's voice never left me alone.

Three days of every week, I worked at Avi's home, but he performed his priestly duties in Jerusalem. I missed his tender advice and considerate conversation. Mary worked with his three daughters every day. When I was at his house, the nanny and cook deferred to me in all things, almost as if I were the mistress of the household.

But I wasn't. And I never would be, no matter how sharply the pang of longing struck my heart. Still, as I dusted the table where Avi's scribing supplies awaited his homecoming, I hummed a tune my mother had taught me.

One thing is needful.

I knew dreaming of the impossible wasn't the thing Yeshua meant. Even though daydreaming was my sister's specialty, I knew Yeshua had been talking of something spiritual. I had been spiteful that day, the furthest thing from the godly example set by Mother Sarah.

I confessed my attitude to Yahweh a hundred times. I took an offering to the temple, praying every moment that G-d would forgive me and show me what one thing I was missing from Messiah's teachings. What one thing did my sister possess as she sat among his disciples that I did not as I bustled around serving them all?

A right spirit.

The answer came to me on the third Sabbath after the embarrassing moment in my home. We'd journeyed to Jerusalem for the Sabbath. I'd offered my doves, my chest aching as I wrung their necks and watched their innocent blood leak into the pot.

"Confess your sins to the Lord, child," the priest said. *Child?* Although he was at least a decade younger than Avi, that meant he was only older than me by the same number of years.

Yahweh, I confess my angry spirit. I am jealous of my younger sister's ability to relax in the presence of Yeshua while I am never content to sit. I want to do things for him. For You. Is it wrong to do things rather than sit at his feet? I know my attitude has not been the best. Forgive me.

As the blood poured out, a gentle caress breathed onto my wounded heart and soul. *G-d's breath.* He'd heard my prayer. He accepted my offering and forgave me.

Tears sprang forth, stinging my nose and wetting my eyes. I lowered my face and drew my shawl closer, pressing its edges against my wet cheeks.

Thank you, G-d of Abraham, Isaac, and Jacob. Show me how to embrace the one thing, the right spirit.

I wish I could say things were much easier after that, but that's not how life works. Not for me, anyway.

Laz brought home another betrothal request for Mary, this one from a man in the merchant's guild. His oldest son had secured a trade route and had put away a goodly sum. He offered regular deliveries of weaving cloth and a monthly payment for Mary's bride price. In exchange, he wanted to marry her before the summer trading season was in full swing.

I knew David the merchant. I was aware of his son Gil, whose interest in Mary had manifested during Pesach[1] two years before. We'd been sharing Seder[2] at cousin Nathan's home, and Gil stopped by the next day. His eyes studied Mary, who worked beside me at the loom, with undisguised covetousness. He'd asked for an introduction from Nathan and then tried to speak with Mary alone.

I wasn't fooled. The man cared only for prospering himself and his business. He would work Mary at the loom like a slave. His offer for her hand was a veiled bribe, as if he knew we couldn't afford to provide a respectable dowry for our sister.

"We should ask Mary if she's interested." Laz took the scroll back from me.

I shook my head. "He is not a godly man."

"You cannot know that." Perspiration beaded his forehead, and he melted into the cushion.

"I've seen the way he looks at her." I stood. "And his offer is laughable."

"He requires no dowry from Mary. How many others will ask the same?"

"To bind her. The dowry is for her protection if he doesn't provide for her."

Laz wiped his forehead. "I won't argue. We'll ask her."

"The decision lies with you." The unfairness of it welled within me. Perhaps I should rejoice that no man wished to buy me like a goat.

"I will consider her wishes, but it won't be the final decision." He rose. "My head aches. I'm going to lie down."

I should have offered him some bark tea, knowing it often helped with aches and pains, but I let him leave. I stomped around the kitchen for a few minutes, sweeping and then beginning the meal preparation.

How quickly I forgot my pledge to have a right spirit!

Later, Mary confirmed that she wasn't interested in Gil Ben-David. "He makes me feel uncomfortable." She stared at her hands. "I love another."

I knew she spoke of Yeshua. "Mary." The brush stilled in my hand. "Yeshua will never marry."

She nodded. A tear rolled down her smooth cheek. I brushed out her silken hair, and she dabbed at her face with the edge of her sleeping shift.

"So you say, but how will I be content to marry another?"

"Because you want a home and family." Isn't that what all of us wanted? I did. I pushed away the selfish pity that tried to rise. This conversation with my sister was more needful than feeling sorry for myself.

The bristles crackled against her locks.

"But there is no one like him." Her tone was wistful but resigned.

I knew it was true, but I was certain he wouldn't want her pining for him. I bent and kissed her cheek before whispering in her ear, "You will know when the right one offers."

After she brushed my hair, we prayed together. She hugged me tightly. "Thank you for praying for me. You're the best sister."

As I write these words, her gratitude is a gift from Yahweh. Finally, I have blessed my sister the way she blesses so many others. For this moment, I know I chose the one needful thing.

Thank you, Yeshua, for being patient with me. When I saw him again, I hoped he'd notice the difference.

My brother's fever raged. Every bad memory from the worst weeks of my life suffocated me. The overripe scent of sickness permeated everything, no matter how often I scrubbed. Still, I swept and cooked and worked for the wealthy who kept food on our table.

Before and after work, I bathed Laz's face with water and rolled him from side to side so I could place clean linen beneath him. Caring for him was a labor of love.

But nothing I did made a difference. His shriveled arm clung to his side like a poultry wing. Muscles in his shorter leg twitched, dislodging the sheepskins I'd heaped over him with hopes it would break the fever. He thrashed and moaned, and it was like seeing the poliomyelitis take my other brother all over again.

Yahweh, I cannot lose another brother.

Watching two people I loved die nearly broke me, and that epidemic did ruin my family. I recalled the way Abba faded away afterward, losing his will to outlive his heir and the woman he loved.

Although he was a cripple, Laz was the only protector Mary and I had. Though he'd never been strong, he was a G-d-fearing man of legal age who kept the meddlers at bay. Everyone knew I was the one that provided for our family. Laz has become a good manager, though, and he'd been handling the scheduling and payments for many years. How would I run the business alone? Especially now that Mary was marriageable and desirable. Unlike me.

Stop feeling pitiful and start being helpful, Mother's voice echoed in my mind.

"I'll sit with him." Mary's soft pledge barely pulled me back to the present.

The huge tears hanging on the edge of her thick lashes

wrenched my heart from my chest. She had lost as much as me, and she felt everything more deeply. If I expected to fold beneath the weight of losing my brother, what would happen to her?

That's when I decided.

"I am sending a message to Yeshua."

Her lips tilted into the closest thing to a smile I'd seen since this fever put Laz abed.

"He can heal anyone." I knew more than faith shone in her glowing gold-flecked eyes, but I ignored it.

Instead, I nodded my agreement. We weren't like so many others who followed Yeshua because of his miracles. He spoke God's Word with authority, and we knew he was Messiah. We'd seen him perform a few feats of divinity, but we'd heard about even more. Blind men saw, and lame men walked. The paralyzed could move, a lad's lunch fed a multitude, and lepers were cleansed.

Whatever afflicted my brother would be a simple matter for the Lord to cure. And we were his friends. He'd done greater things for strangers. Surely he wouldn't begrudge this small favor to friends?

I scrounged around for a scrap of parchment and scratched a short message. *The one you love is ill.* I signed it: *Martha and Mary.*

After tying my coin purse to my sash and covering my head with a shawl, I strode toward the well. Many of the orphan boys spent their afternoons in the shade abutting the common area. I thought I knew where Yeshua and his disciples planned to teach, and if I got the fastest messenger, the

Lord could come and touch Laz. This sickness would be over, and our lives could get back to normal.

In a grove of fig trees by the well, a group of youths tossed bean bags back and forth. The scent of baking bread from the community oven a little farther down the rutted road reminded my stomach that I had neglected to eat. There'd been too much to accomplish, or at least I didn't wish to sit still for more than a minute because then the grief crashed over me.

I saw one of the orphans who slept at the synagogue and assisted the rabbis.

"Jonathon."

After he sent the bean bag across the circle to another boy, he jogged over. His yellowing smile revealed two gaps on opposite sides of his front teeth.

"Miss Martha."

I asked if he could run into Galilee, and of course he answered, "If the price is right."

I squinted at his face. He didn't flinch from my searching gaze. This one might have been a thief if the rabbi hadn't taken an interest in him, but his quickness suited me at the moment.

After we agreed on a price, I paid him half of the coins and handed him the rolled parchment.

"It's important that you find Yeshua of Nazareth right away." *My brother's life depends on it.*

He tucked the coins and message into a pocket Mary had sewn into his robe for this very purpose and sprinted toward the synagogue.

At Avi's house, I scrubbed floors, washed dirty linens and hung them when they were clean. All the while, I alternated between praying for my brother and praying for Jonathan to reach the Lord quickly. I estimated how much time it would take the boy to reach Capernaum. He was quick and could run for hours but was only a lad.

If he reached Jesus in two days, and Jesus came immediately, it would still be four days until they arrived. I groaned.

Yahweh, my brother needs your help. His fever will take him before Messiah arrives. Please, spare him.

And so the hours were spent.

When I arrived home, back aching and hands pruned from too much contact with filthy water, Mary didn't greet me. I hurried behind the curtain to my brother's private sleeping area.

Mary's face was streaked with tears. My heart dropped to the floor a beat before I fell to my knees beside Laz's pallet.

His thin chest rose. His clammy face was paler than it had been in the morning.

"Run, get more cold water." I saw the jar beside her wasn't empty, but I needed to do something.

"He's worse." Emotion gummed up her words.

"Why do you say that?" I soaked a linen strip in the tepid water.

"He stopped thrashing about an hour ago."

"Peaceful sleep will help him heal." My stomach tied itself in a knot. It didn't believe my words.

After a few moments during which my sister sniffled and

I bathed my brother's face, Mary left the room. She returned with a bowl to pour the water in, then she left the house with the water jug.

Yahweh, let this be a healing sleep.

But the churning stew in my stomach splashed onto my heart. My chest ached with a fearful certainty.

Doubt whispered about my long-dead family. *You prayed then too*, it taunted.

Behind my closed eyelids, the morning of Grandmother's death replayed. She'd called for me. I heard her frail voice: *Martha, help me*. But I'd turned my back to the call, so tired and wanting nothing but sleep.

It was Mary who found her later that morning. Eyes and mouth open, as if she still called out for me. I'd had nightmares about it for months.

Lord, you have forgiven me. I promised to take care of Laz and Mary. Help us.

Laz took a shuddering breath and moaned quietly.

Please let Yeshua come soon.

MY TWENTY-FOURTH WINTER

On the third morning after I sent Yeshua the message, I woke with a start. The old dream had revisited me, and I listened for my grandmother and heard her calling my name. But the more I listened, the more I heard nothing but my gasping, speeding breath.

Yesterday's pain swept over me. Lazarus had morphed from a sweating mess that could hardly swallow water to a still, grayish near-corpse. When I fell asleep with an urgent prayer to our G-d on my lips, my brother had still been alive.

I stared around the room, telling myself it was the nightmare that awakened me.

A nightmare based on the truth. My grandmother had called for me the morning she died, but I ignored her plea. I turned my back on the doorway to her room and faded back into sleep.

Today, I wouldn't make the same mistake. I bolted

upright, held my breath and listened, but the only noises were a barking dog and bleating goat from outside. The bed beside me remained empty.

Sometime in the night, Mary shooed me from Laz's room and made herself comfortable on the pallet beside our brother.

"I'm younger." She hadn't bothered to whisper.

Both of us feared our brother was beyond waking now.

Yeshua, please come. Lord G-d of Abraham, have mercy. Send him to us.

My heart pounded and my gut clenched as I hurried through my morning ablutions. I sidled into the other room where Mary lay curled on a rug beside the bed. My knees jostled the pallet as I squeezed to the other side of my brother's bed. I stared at his chest, and finally it raised the wool blanket a smidgen. His forehead felt dry but not especially hot beneath my palm.

As I leaned over to wet and wring a strip of linen from the pot of water, Mary stirred. Her eyes followed my movement. While I bathed Laz's face, she hurried out with the jug, and I heard her sandals snap against the packed floor.

"You've slept enough, lazy Laz." I tried to smile when I used the old nickname.

Several years before the epidemic sapped his strength and shriveled his arm and leg, he had invented it to tease me. I'd tell him to do something, and he'd reply, "Lazy Laz would rather not." Then laugh when I got angry.

My lips twitched at the memory of Laz happy and whole. It had been so long ago.

Another lifetime.

"Yeshua will be here soon." ***Please, G-d, make it true***. "What will he say if you're still abed?"

I patted his gaunt, sunken cheek, as Grandmother had done the few times I'd been ill. Laz hadn't looked so near death for many years. The nightmarish days of the plague reared into my mind, and I gagged, nearly bringing bread up from my stomach.

I gulped air to soothe the sick feeling in my gut. I blinked and tried to pray. No words came. My chest ached, and an emptiness devoured me from the inside. My well of faith had drained away.

I don't know how many times I'd bathed his face before Mary spelled me so I could go to work. Work had always been my refuge, but not these days. Nothing diverted my mind from the state of Lazarus.

Yahweh, help my family. Heal my brother. Bring Yeshua to Bethany soon.

Hours dragged like a chastised child drug his feet. When the messenger came, I was scrubbing Avi's cobbled floors.

I recognized the boy as one who lived a few houses from us.

"You must come," he said. "Your brother is worse."

My heart choked me. I slipped the boy a penny and swallowed back my tears, struggling to heave the wash pot where I'd been rinsing my scrub brush.

Avi stepped from his office and rested a hand on my shoulder. The warmth of his simple touch filled me with an indescribable ache. I wished he would hold me as I had held

Mary when she'd found Grandmother dead in bed all those years ago.

He's not dead yet. I tried to stiffen my spine, but everything ached.

"Go. I'll empty your vessel." Avi's brown eyes held compassion so like Yeshua's. "Be with your family. I will send Imma with a meal."

My yearning for him surged. I wanted to feel strong arms, as I often had when my father lived. But Avi was not my father, and there was no one to comfort me now.

"Thank you."

"Let me know what you need." His voice was firm. These weren't the empty words of a neighbor trying to put you off while saying the expected helpful phrases.

My heart swelled so much I couldn't speak, could barely breathe. I nodded. When his hand dropped, I shivered, missing it, but turned quickly and rushed away, embarrassed by my neediness.

Yahweh, help me. Raise Laz from his sick bed. Please, send Yeshua to heal him.

I rushed blindly through the familiar streets, my heart pleading for a miracle. Finally, I made it to my brother's bedside where Mary knelt, bathing his face with a cloth. His shallow breaths barely moved his blankets. He moaned and gasped.

Then all was still. Time stopped. Mary's eyes widened, and she looked at me with a desperate plea.

I shuffled around her and shook our brother's shoulders. "Lazarus. Wake up."

The blankets dislodged from his skeletal chest. I pulled the cloth away from his gray, clammy face. Still, he didn't move. No warm breath stirred against the palm I held before his nose and mouth.

"No. Yahweh, no." The words croaked from my tight throat.

Why, G-d?

I sucked air into my heaving lungs. I needed to be strong. *As always.*

I laid a hand on Mary's shoulder, willing it to comfort her. "He's gone." The last word mocked me with its truthfulness.

Mary wailed and crumpled across Laz. Her weeping cracked the wall I'd erected the day my father died. Pain scalded, bubbling from the hidden room within my soul. Tears washed my face, but they couldn't scour away my questions.

"Why, Lord? I don't understand."

Our father Job asked why, but God never answered him. The rabbi's words, spoken when I'd asked him why Abba died, echoed inside me.

But Yeshua could have come and saved my brother. I kept these words inside. Would I blame our friend for letting Laz die?

I shook my head. Liquid pain poured from my eyes and nose. I rubbed Mary's back as I had when she was a child in need of comfort. Her thin frame shook the bed, and her wails echoed my agony.

My other hand rested on Laz's forehead. My brother was gone. He was in the bosom of Father Abraham now—that's what the rabbi would say. Now, Laz was comforted and whole. I should have been happy for him, but my heart broke at the sounds of my sister's sobs, and an emptiness I had never completely forgotten smothered me.

I hadn't been able to protect my little brother from sickness. And because of that, Mary and I were two women alone in a world where men were supposed to protect and care for us. Men like Yeshua. Men like Avi. And even men like Laz.

A guttural moan pushed free from my chest. My tears fell faster.

After Mother died, Abba had asked me to take care of Laz and Mary. *They need you, Martha*, he'd told me.

I promise to take care of them, Abba. That's what I'd told him. I'd reiterated the pledge the day he died.

Today I'd failed him. I'd failed everyone.

7

MY TWENTY-FOURTH WINTER

*M*y eyes burned like the coals of our cooking fire, and a headache throbbed behind them as if straining to break from the sides of my head. Avi's cook Imma hummed the mourning psalm again. I'd lost track of how many times she'd started it, but I still didn't feel more than a tad guilty that I'd asked her to stop singing the words. How long ago had that been?

The slant of the sun no longer lightened the window, and our huddled group of mourners were draped in shadows that matched the tone of the day and every tunic and veil in the room.

Four days. Seven days since I'd sent Jonathon with a message for Yeshua.

As if thinking of the boy brought him, he slipped through the lambskin that covered the doorway. After pausing a moment, he sidled against my arm. The scent of fish swirled around him, and I wondered what he'd been up to.

Then guilt plunged into my heart. How could I wonder something so mundane when my brother was dead?

"The Master comes." His whisper burned along my cheekbone.

I pressed my veil over my mouth to subdue a gasp. *Finally.* It was too late for Laz.

A sob tried to catch in my throat at the thought of my baby brother, wrapped in linen and settled on the shelf in our family's burial cave. I swallowed it. Hadn't I cried enough tears to flood our home?

But Yeshua could comfort Mary.

As I stood, Imma glanced at me. I gestured toward Mary and Avi's two older daughters. The girls clung to my sister, whose face was shrouded behind a mourning veil. Periodically, her sobs would spur the crowd around her to wail and rock, but at the moment her shoulders stooped. Her downcast gaze seemed to be pinned to the scrap of cloth clutched in her hands. Cloth she'd cut from Laz's robe the day he died.

I gripped the side of my tunic and swallowed the emotion welling in my throat.

Yeshua is here. He will help.

An ember of anger thrummed to life in my chest. Why hadn't Yeshua come sooner? Then I chastised myself. Yeshua had more important things to do than heal one insignificant man.

But he was everything to Mary and me.

I followed Jonathon through the doorway, blinking away

tears that formed at the brightness of the day. The sun continued to shine. It cared nothing for the loss imploding my world. But the Master should have cared. Laz had been a friend to him, and even more, he'd been a vocal supporter of Yeshua as Messiah.

I pushed at the selfish thoughts trying to surface. Memories of scrubbing and serving, everything to make Yeshua comfortable because his ministry took him far from the comforts of home. He'd warned me not to focus on what I could do for him. *Mary has chosen that good part, which shall not be taken away from her.*

Yes, Lord, I know. My gift is different than my sister's, and worldly responsibilities take too much of my focus.

Somehow, the admission did more to push away my anger than anything else.

Dust puffed around Jonathon's scurrying feet. I pressed my veil tighter, blinking back more moisture. I would not cry when I saw Yeshua, but I wouldn't avoid the topic of Laz's sickness and death. The Master never discouraged me from being straightforward with him, as long as sharp words were tempered with loving kindness.

Could I do that in my current emotional state? I didn't know.

So, I prayed as we left the rutted path and trotted through the narrow streets of town. We'd barely reached the western outskirts when I saw the group of dust-covered disciples. Yeshua looked up and stepped away from the others.

"Thank you." I patted the boy's shoulder, and he sprinted

back toward town, probably looking for someone who would pay him for running a message. I hadn't thought to grab a coin for him.

Yeshua stopped an arm's length from me. The lines in his face deepened. Emotion stirred in the depths of his dark eyes.

I dipped my head and stared at his filthy toes. Emotions I couldn't identify roiled in my stomach, and I wanted to scream.

G-d, You know all things. You know I prayed. Help me now. I don't blame Yeshua for Laz's death. I took a deep breath and closed my eyes. ***I don't.***

I swallowed again, coaxing my scratchy throat to work. "Lord, if you had been here, my brother would not have died[1]."

The last word broke as sorrow swelled from deep within my aching soul.

No tears. For once, my eyes remained dry, and the words came out as more of a statement and less of an accusation.

Is that what I intended?

I raised my eyes to look at Yeshua. His gaze hadn't moved from my face. I swallowed. "I know that even now, whatever you ask of G-d, G-d will give it thee[2]."

What did I hope he'd ask? That G-d would grant supernatural comfort to Mary, who'd been shaking apart at the seams these past days? She'd wanted him to come and heal her brother.

We'd wanted him to come. But now, it was too late.

Yeshua sighed. I dove into the compassionate gaze that had first drawn me to him.

"Your brother shall rise again[3]."

My heart leapt. The pounding made it difficult to swallow. Would he bring Laz back to life? I shook away that foolish hope. Why would I think that? Everyone had an appointment with death, and Laz had been living on borrowed time for most of his life.

I gulped down the conflicting emotions. "I know he shall rise again in the resurrection at the last day[4]."

Those foolish Sadducees might ignore the resurrection, but I had been listening as Yeshua taught his disciples. This life was short, but Messiah granted eternal life in Paradise with Father Abraham, Isaac, and Jacob.

That hope brought a small measure of comfort, but couldn't G-d offer us more than that?

Yeshua shuffled a half step closer. "I am the resurrection, and the life. He that believes in me." He gestured toward the disciples. He could have been motioning toward the graveyard, although I hadn't considered that at the time. "Though he were dead, yet shall he live[5]."

I nodded. The hole in my heart I had hoped he would mend gaped. Futility washed through me. My siblings were my responsibility, and now only one remained, and her heart was broken beyond repair.

He continued to speak. "And whoever lives and believes in me shall never die."

What? Laz believed more than anyone I knew, and he was dead. I'd been the one to wash his lifeless flesh and wrap it in strips of linen. Tears tried to choke me again.

Those compassionate brown eyes full of love and kindness bored into my anxious heart. "Do you believe this[6]?"

Conflicting emotions roiled beneath my malfunctioning lungs. I couldn't breathe for an instant. Darkness flashed along the edges of my vision.

Yahweh, you know I believe.

As soon as the prayer fluttered from my heart, air rushed into my lungs. I coughed slightly, covering my mouth with the black veil to keep dust from irritating me.

I nodded. "Yes, Lord. I believe you are the Christ, the Son of G-d, which should come into the world[7]."

At my confession, something lifted inside me. I still wanted to weep, but I no longer thought I would crumble into a thousand pieces.

His eyes sobered, and he turned toward the crowd of disciples who passed a water skin around, talking in low voices. Andrew bar Jonas caught my eye, touching his fingers to his forehead in a show of respect.

The peace I'd come seeking warred with unmet expectations. Laz was still dead, but Yeshua was Messiah, so there was hope. He would make things right. Somehow. I trotted back toward the house.

Mary needed this peace more than I. Why hadn't I brought her with me?

Realization struck me. I'd been thinking I might have a confrontation with Yeshua. However, one look in his eyes, and I knew he experienced the same sorrow we did.

Mary would see it too, and that commiseration would be its own form of comfort.

8

MY TWENTY-FOURTH WINTER

I slipped into the house. Several heads turned in my direction as I paused inside the threshold.

Once my eyes adjusted, I circled around the knot of women and stood behind my little sister. She'd grown up so much in the two years we'd followed Yeshua's ministry, but she seemed small and frail with Avi's daughters huddled into her side.

I couldn't take care of Laz anymore, but I could make sure Mary found comfort. She needed to see Yeshua. Speaking to him had comforted me, and her tender heart suffered more than mine.

I pressed my hand into her shoulder and tugged her toward the linen that partitioned off Laz's sleeping space.

Imma glanced up with wide eyes, and I nodded toward the two girls who clung to Mary's sides. The old cook scurried over to hug them into her ample sides.

Mary stumbled to her feet as I tugged her into the tiny bedroom. Even with fresh straw, the bed where our brother passed into the next life screamed grief into the silence.

In a hushed voice I told her, "The Master has come and calls for you[1]."

Another twinge tugged where my heart used to be whole.

Yahweh, forgive the little untruth.

He assured me that there was only truth or lies, no sizable ones of either.

Forgive this lie, then. I justified it in my mind with, *I'm trying to help her find peace.*

I sensed G-d wasn't impressed with my reasoning. My sister's face sparked to life, so I could push the niggle of guilt to the back of my mind.

Mary gasped. "Where?"

"I'll show you."

We weaved through the crush of mourners with her hand pressed into mine. Voices rose to mutters and exclamations.

"Where are you going?" Imma caught my arm, but I swept her hold away and rushed toward the door.

Someone said, "She's going to the grave to weep[2]."

Let them think what they would.

I squeezed my sister's hand and led her toward Yeshua's circle of followers. As we neared, he broke away, looking more crestfallen than when I'd left him.

Mary wobbled, and I dropped her hand.

She crumpled into a heap near Yeshua's feet. He would pick her up. He was here now, and I relinquished control to him.

Behind me, I heard the rustle of fabric and plod of footsteps. Imma followed us, an arm slung around the shoulders
of Avi's girls. Behind her came a black-shrouded clot of
women, our comforters.

"Lord," my sister cried, "if you had been here, my brother
would not have died[3]."

My throat ached, straining to hold back tears. I'd said the
same thing to Yeshua, but the pain that broke my sister's voice
made the accusatory words an admission of her heartache
rather than his shortcomings. Faith and love met with
confusion.

Why hadn't he come when we told him Lazarus was sick?

Yeshua glanced at her, then up at me and finally toward
the crowd of women. Our group hadn't gone through town
unseen, and many of them were joined by their husbands.

Yeshua bent and touched my sister's shoulder. Her
indrawn gasp turned into a sob. He guided her to her feet,
gently, like a father helping an injured child.

Please let his touch have Heavenly comfort.

By the time she stood, his face was marred by the anguish
scarring my heart. His gaze met mine.

"Where have you laid him?"

From behind me, one of the men who'd helped us carry
Laz to his tomb came forward. "Come and see."

Our procession continued down the dusty road and cut
onto a narrower path. It was then, as Mary leaned against my
side, sopping tears from her face with her veil, that I realized
Yeshua could have been pointing to the grave during our
conversation.

Something buzzed in the abyss where the monster of loss lurked after devouring my heart and half my soul. Something I didn't recognize because I hadn't truly allowed myself to feel it since Mother and the others had died.

I stopped several feet from the tomb, a step behind Yeshua. His shoulders shook, and I realized he was weeping. A moan hiccupped inside me, but I swallowed it. Mary leaned into me like a weary animal.

I knew he had loved my brother. Some in the crowd muttered that very thing.

Why then hadn't he come and healed him?

Don't doubt. Just believe.

Yahweh, help me believe in Your perfect will.

Mary blinked at the Lord, finally understanding that he was crying. Her fingers lifted in his direction, and then she clenched her skirt.

"Couldn't this man who opened the eyes of the blind have kept this man from dying?[4]" a man from the crowd asked, and I knew his voice carried to Yeshua.

Others agreed, muttering among themselves. I wanted to hush them, but I stiffened and continued to pray. My arm tightened around Mary, and she melded to my side. She sniffed, but for the first time in days, she wasn't trembling from grief.

Thank you, G-d of Abraham for strengthening her.

Yeshua stepped forward. Several of his disciples exchanged glances. What was going on?

He came within touching distance of the cave where Lazarus was buried beside our father.

"Take away the stone."

MY TWENTY-FOURTH WINTER

He couldn't mean that. Could he?

"Lord, by this time he stinks." It was my voice that stated the obvious. "He's been dead four days[1]."

Surely, he wouldn't think of viewing the body at this late time?

Yeshua turned toward me, eyes red from his weeping, but his voice was strong, carrying to the crowd behind us. "Didn't I say you would see the glory of God if you would believe?[2]"

His words slapped me into silence. I did believe he was Messiah. I did trust him to do what was best. Why did I question what he did then?

I dropped my eyes.

Forgive me.

Several of the disciples scuffled to the cave and lifted the stone.

Yeshua looked toward Heaven. "Father, I thank thee that Thou hast heard me."

As his authoritative voice rose, the muttering crowd around us went silent.

"I know Thou hears me always, but because of the people which stand by I said it, that they may believe that Thou hast sent me.[3]"

Such simple, conviction-filled words lent power to prayer. When would I learn to pray with assurance that Yahweh heard me and wanted to respond, as a father with a child?

The crowd shifted. Everyone focused on the gaping hole in the side of the hill that held the body of my brother.

"Lazarus," Yeshua's voice rang out, "come forth[4]."

Everything stopped. I held my breath, even as the air around me stilled, the wind itself afraid to blow until Yeshua's command had been obeyed.

Rustling sounded from the cave. Mary gasped, quickly silencing herself with a hand over her mouth. A form waddled through the gaping crack. Linen strips I had cut bound him, so he could barely move. Even his face was covered.

Lazarus? Was it possible Yeshua had given me exactly what my heart desired when I'd met him on the road? Had he known my unspoken request?

The foreign emotion burning in my stomach ignited through my chest. I couldn't breathe, and dark spots danced around my vision.

Yeshua gestured to the stunned disciples, frozen beside the stone they'd carried. "Loose him."

"He's alive?" Mary twisted in my arms. I squinted to see her wide eyes behind the dark veil.

My voice refused to obey me, so I nodded. She flung herself against my chest, and I hugged her with arms that felt as if they belonged to someone else. Even my knees felt shaky.

Yahweh, I had no faith.

I hadn't expected to see my brother again. Not in this life.

One of the disciples cut the knots holding Laz's hands to his body. Another worked on the strips of cloth binding his knees and feet together. Mary and I gaped at the unfolding miracle.

A week ago, we'd asked the Lord to come help our brother. Today, we hadn't asked for anything, but Yeshua had known our secret desires.

Yeshua is Messiah. Messiah is God's Anointed.

Once the strips were cut, Mary and I rushed forward.

"Enough." I put my hand on Simon Peter's, pressing the knife away from the cloth. If he kept cutting, Laz would be as naked as a babe before the crowd.

Mary fell against our brother, whose bare arms raised to hold her. Both arms. The right one was no longer withered and useless, but it was now as whole as the left.

I jerked to face Yeshua. "How?" But my lips had barely formed the word when his hand raised to silence me.

"Give G-d the glory."

"Praise G-d! My brother lives!" The cry echoed from my throat, nearly as loud as Yeshua's cry to Lazarus had been. "Praise G-d for Yeshua, Israel's Messiah."

Shouts of praise echoed around me.

I stumbled forward and embraced my brother and sister. "Laz!"

A laugh gurgled from his chest. He whispered for our ears only, "Lazy Laz is gone forever."

Tears wet my cheeks, and then I joined Laz and Mary in the most heartfelt laughter I'd ever known.

My brother was dead. My brother is alive.

Praise Yahweh. Praise Yeshua.

MY TWENTY-FOURTH WINTER

I should have been grateful. My brother lived again. More than that, he was whole for the first time since he was a child of eight.

But within a week of his miraculous return to life, I realized many things about myself. None of them were good.

It started with his trip to the Weavers' Guild in Jerusalem to seek re-admittance. Although Laz had been unable to weave for more than a decade, he knew how to choose good threads and understood the business side of things. We hadn't been guild members since a few months after Father passed from this world because there wasn't a man to carry on the business.

Now, it seemed, all that would change.

I dragged myself and Mary home that day. She carried the market basket filled with our fruit, nuts, and some vegetables for the meal. I clutched a thin bird from one of the merchants who sometimes requested I clean and organize his shop. It wasn't my favorite job because his wife followed me around and complained about every item I moved.

Still, I'd earned store credit and the bird, one they didn't need for the pot that night. One that would hardly offer three bites for each of the members of my household.

Lord, I'm so ungrateful. Forgive me.

Inside the house, Laz sat with a man who seemed vaguely familiar. He was older than me, and gray threaded his beard. His gaze swept me aside to land on my sister.

So that was the way of things. Well, we'd said no to plenty of suitors before.

Laz rushed forward to take the basket from Mary. His cheeks were flushed, and a light of excitement filled his eyes. Not a good sign, I realized later.

"This is Barta bar Jagur." Laz took Mary's hand. "My sister Mary."

Barta had lurched to his feet when we entered and now stepped forward to lift my sister's fingers and bow slightly. His dark eyes perused her, lingering at her hips before returning to stare hungrily at her lovely face.

"Jagur of the Woolen Guild?" My heart thudded a doomsday march. It couldn't be. Jagur had been no friend of our family, always trying to barter away my mother's artistic creations for pennies. All because she'd spurned him.

Barta ignored me, but Laz nodded, a smile spreading slowly over his face. "Yes. It was good fortune that I ran into him after submitting my request for reinstatement into the Weavers' Guild."

Good fortune? Hardly. My brother had been too young to understand Jagur's machinations, and how the lust for my mother had motivated many of his spiteful actions toward our family. I had been eleven when Mother sat beside me at the loom and explained how some men thought women were playthings.

"That is why Jehovah gave us honorable men like your father," Mother had told me. The words echoed in my ears again. "They protect us from the unholy desires of men like Jagur."

She'd named him without a blink, without fear of retribution from one of the wealthiest, prominent members of a sister guild.

The next time Jagur came to Bethany to inspect the "wares" our family wove, I'd watched and listened. His eyes followed Mother's every move, and although his girth spoke of no missed meals, his look reminded me of the starving street boys when I walked by with fresh bread.

His son looked at my sister with that same unholy desire.

My stomach churned, and I clutched Mary's arm more tightly. She cast a quizzical look in my direction before dropping her eyes to the floor.

I will not let him have her.

Mary and I set about making dinner. Every time I tried to send her outside, Laz gave me a sharp look. So, I stirred the fowl in the pot over the outside fire, constantly asking Mary to bring me another herb, some leeks or more chopped vegetables.

When it was time to bake bread, I pretended the pot

needed stirring and asked her to do the baking. She wrinkled her forehead, perplexed by my machinations. Her innocent reaction reminded me exactly why I needed to look out for her.

Outside, we could finally speak freely. "He is not a good man," I whispered to her.

"I am not interested in marrying him." Of course, she wasn't. She still had her heart set on the impossible.

I kept stirring. She turned the bread on the cooking stone.

"You're not going to tell me I'm wrong."

I sighed. "You've heard what I have to say about that."

We finished the meal preparations. I doubled up the edging of my shawl to heft the pot from the fire. Mary's hand on mine gave me pause.

Her brown eyes were wide as she asked, "Laz won't force me to marry him, will he?"

I blinked at her. "Of course not."

But the way Laz scraped and bowed made me wonder. All during dinner, Barta gloated about the fine wools he'd contracted from Persians and Syrians. He couldn't say enough about the rare dyes he used to make royal blue and deep maroon and even gold-tinted yarns for weaving.

"These yarns might even be worthy of an artist as skilled as you." He gazed at Mary. The words he spoke were complimentary and truthful, but the lust in his eyes said her talent was the secondary reason he bid for her hand in marriage.

The fowl I'd swallowed turned to coal, burning my stomach. I clenched my hands in my lap, afraid I might toss the liquid in my half-full cup into his face.

My sister hadn't lifted her eyes above his chin during the entire meal. Even then, when all of us paused to gape at her, it took a moment before she realized he'd spoken to her.

"Martha has the finest skills." She gestured toward me, her fingers trembling slightly as she picked up her cup.

The red wine was much stronger than we ever drank. The drink had been Barta's gift for the meal, and only a rude hostess would turn it away. I could hardly wait for him to leave so I could water it down. Once diluted, we could drink that wine for a week or more.

"But you're the one who teaches the skill to Avi the priest's daughters. Your work is what decorates your cousin's study."

Nathan's study. I should have guessed Jagur's son would frequent it. Mary had crafted our cousin a fine rug the previous year as a gift when we'd stayed over for several of the feast days. He'd pushed her to show him the pattern on his loom, thinking that was the best form of gratitude he could offer.

I shook my head. "Without a weaver, we had to sell our largest loom." My voice was colder than midwinter.

"I assure you, looms and the finest quality wool won't be a problem in the future." Even as he replied to me, Barta's longing gaze never strayed from my sister's face.

It seemed like hours before he left. I slammed around the kitchen, cleaning like a devil would steal my soul if I left a speck of dust anywhere. Mary scraped the bowls and cups with ashes from the fire outside.

"I don't care what he offered." I faced Laz. My fingertips

dug into my hips, and I imagined my lovely mother looking fearsome in a similar pose.

"What is your objection?"

"He looks at Mary with open lust."

"She's a lovely woman. Many men desire her." Laz crossed his arms over his chest. My gaze fell on his formerly withered arm, now equal in size and strength to the other.

Yahweh, I wish You'd never healed him.

And my heart ached at that compulsive prayer because even now, I know I meant it. Being whole had changed my brother and not in a way that was best for our family.

"All the more reason for her to marry." I'd seen the set of that chin often enough on Abba.

"Not to a man who only wants one thing from her."

My brother scowled. "You heard him praise her work. He recognized her weaving skills."

"He'll work her like a slave during the day and at night—" I gulped at the thought, and the accusation stuck in my throat. As a maiden, what did I really know about what happened in a marriage bed at night?

"It's not up to you."

My chin rose. "You're right. It's up to her."

Laz shook his head, and his shoulders slumped. "I don't want to fight, Martha. His offer is much better than anything I could have imagined."

"You'll sell your sister? Like she's a slave?"

"She's not a slave!"

Mary entered, stopping our battle of words. The curtain flopped over the doorway. She tossed her headscarf onto the table in front of us, and the dishes she carried thumped after the fabric.

"Why do you discuss me like a child?" Hurt filled her eyes with tears. She glanced first at Laz and then at me.

I reached out, wanting to comfort her, but she stepped back. Her movement caused a fist to squeeze my heart.

"Is it up to me whom I marry?" Her voice rang with something I'd never heard from her. Something that sounded like determination.

Laz sighed. "I want to discuss it with you, yes. But you should visit his house in the city first."

"His house doesn't matter to me."

Laz stepped around the table, so sure with two strong legs. Mary sidled backward, but his hands captured her shoulders to keep her from fleeing.

"It should. He would make a good husband." Something tender passed between my siblings. Laz loved her. "He offers the best of everything to you, and your future sons and daughters."

Tears carved paths down her flaming cheeks. "Everything? Does he love G-d? Does he believe in Yeshua?"

Laz huffed. "Your faith will be passed to your sons and daughters."

"But I had a father with strong faith. That's what I want for my children."

While my own heart ached, knowing I would never bear children, Mary knew she would. After fourteen springs, she was lovelier than the lilies on the mountains. Even if she turned away this wealthy suitor, another man would offer for her hand. One that loved G-d like she did.

"I want you to think about this."

Mary shook her head. Her face crumpled, and the moment Laz removed his hands, she bolted for our room. Not that the piece of linen hanging over the doorway offered much privacy.

Something seemed wrong about Laz's determination to accept this offer. Why was he so determined she would accept Barta bar Jagur when he'd refused so many others?

I narrowed my eyes at him. "What did he offer, Lazarus?"

My brother started. I didn't use his full name if we were home alone. "An apprenticeship in the Scrivener's Guild." He wiped his face. "For me."

A mentorship to be a scribe? I should have guessed. My brother could weave and run a business, but words had always made his heart run over with joy. Reading had always been his greatest love, and having a useless arm had made writing difficult but not impossible. Except no one wanted to apprentice him because he had no connections, and now he was too old to begin an apprenticeship.

But the lusts of Barta bar Jagur drove him to spend and barter favors. It disgusted me that wealth could purchase what honor could not.

Why, Lord? Why does it have to be this way?

"Avi would find you a mentor. You don't have to sell Mary for that."

"Barta isn't a bad man."

I shook my head. My brother never saw the raw side of humanity. He wanted to believe the best, so he did.

"I want to talk to her alone."

Laz nodded at my request, went to his room, and returned with a couple of scrolls. There was enough daylight left for him to read elsewhere.

Once he was gone, I returned the dishes to their shelf and made certain everything was tidy for the following morning. I leaned against the counter and sighed.

Yahweh help me have the right words for my sister.

Familiar peace swept over me, gentle as a dew-filled breeze. I stayed in that position long enough to calm my racing heart and relax my tense shoulders. Why did supplication always seem to be my last step instead of my first?

Forgive me, Yahweh. Yeshua says we need to be wise as serpents.

And harmless as doves. The rest of Messiah's teaching rang through me, his voice clear.

In our room, Mary huddled in the middle of the bed. Her shoulders weren't shaking, but I could hear her stuffy breathing. She'd already cried herself out.

I sat beside her. After several long minutes, she rolled onto her back and stared at me. The sight of her puffy eyes and swollen face tore the rest of the hardness from my heart.

"I agree that Barta bar Jagur is not a good match for you, but you must promise me you will consider other men Laz talks to." *Yeshua will never take a wife.*

"Why must I marry?"

"You need a man to protect you."

She blinked. "You're not married."

My chest crumpled onto my heart like a building falling on a baby bird. I gasped for breath, cupping the center of my chest.

"I must take care of you and Laz." I could hear Abba's final exhortation ringing through my mind.

"It seems like Laz has returned from the dead to take his place at the head of the family." Her voice was hoarse, barely a whisper.

The words were a knife. All these years, I'd done my best for my siblings, but I was easily replaced by a man.

Yahweh, it's so unfair.

I wish You'd never healed Him. My thoughts from earlier echoed back at me.

The pain in my chest escalated.

"Mary, you must find a husband because you are beautiful and desirable. Men won't stop asking after you until you're married."

"I wish they would."

She snatched her journal and quill from beside her pillow. I curled my feet beneath me so she could get past. I understood her desire for time alone, time to process everything that had happened.

I sat on our bed. Sweat dripped down my back. I thought, and I prayed, but I had to wait to process everything until my sister returned with the quill we shared.

As I write these words, I think I've done nothing but brood.

Each time I try to pray, I find that I'm a little bit angry that the G-d of Abraham gave me responsibility and then jerked it away.

It's late before I can finally pray with sincerity.

Yahweh, forgive me. Your plan is perfect. Help me trust it like I trust You.

Sleep still didn't come easily. I would regret that the next morning.

MY TWENTY-FOURTH SPRING

As I hurried to leave for work, I dropped a bundle of filthy clothes beside Mary. She sat on our bed cradling Grandmother's ornate box of spikenard. It rested in her palms like a priceless jewel, and it was worth more than anything else in our home.

"I'm going to do it." Her soft words froze me.

I tensed for an argument, wanting her to keep the box for her wedding. Tears glistened in her eyes and on her lashes.

"To thank him." The strangled whisper gutted me like a hapless fish.

I didn't need to ask why she wanted to thank Yeshua. There were so many reasons, and he deserved more than lip service.

"Mary." My voice was husky, and I tried to clear the thickness from my throat. "The elders seek to destroy him." This was Laz's latest news from Jerusalem.

Since his resurrection, our brother had been a celebrity in town and in wider circles. Since his healing, he'd spent much of his time in the Guild District planning to begin our father's business anew now that he had two good hands. The leaders of the guild were trying to convince him to work as a mentor in Jerusalem. I suspected they only wanted to profit from his fame, although I doubted that celebrity status would last much longer. There's always some other great thing to attract people's attention.

I swallowed the rest of my argument. *I'm sorry, Grandmother, but I gave the ointment to her. She can use it as she wants.*

I pulled Mary to my chest for a brief hug. Her strong, slender arms returned the embrace. After covering my head, I dashed outside. There was much to do before I went to Simon's house to prepare his home for the feast he was holding for Laz.

My brother would sit in the honored seat at the same table as Messiah. I shook my head at the insanity of such a thing. Yes, Laz was alive, and I'd heard his tale of being in Paradise. As amazing as it was, Laz didn't do any of it on his own. Yeshua called my brother from the grave. Shouldn't He be the guest of honor? Was Simon bypassing the Lord because he feared the Council?

The business of the day pushed the thoughts away. In the market, I purchased a tender, doe-eyed ewe, herbs, spices, and a collection of roots and legumes. With Pesach near, some things weren't available, but I'd gotten enough to make a welcome feast, and Simon's regular cook was purchasing the fruit and sweets to finish the meal in fine style.

A breeze cooled the cooking courtyard. I was thankful for the portico over the preparation counters. The cook hummed as she cut and chopped, and I prayed.

Yahweh, I will not worry about this feast. I will trust You to provide the strength and comfort I need to serve.

I thought of Simon's wife. Most women I cared for during malaise became my friends, but not Deborah. Nothing I did was good enough for her, and she resented my strength more than she appreciated how I used it on her behalf. Today, she would be seeking the smallest thing to criticize.

But I am serving You. I am honoring Yeshua and Lazarus and Simon, and I want my heart to be in the right place.

In the shadow of so many preparations, the day sped away. Before I was ready, Deborah strolled through the preparations, glanced in the warming ovens and lingered beside the cook. I steered clear of her, taking the opportunity to splash water on my overheated face and remove the apron I'd used to protect my simple dress while I cooked.

"Come to the dining court." The mistress' tone brooked no disagreement.

I dried my hands on my shawl, which I'd discarded in the cool room hours earlier and then tossed it over my hair. Deborah wouldn't look favorably on an uncovered maiden.

"This is the men's." She paused beside a large rectangular table. Ornate pillows surrounded it. "Simon and Lazarus at his right hand." She sniffed as if my brother's name was malodorous.

Yahweh, I meant what I prayed. Forgive me for this desire to shake her.

Or slap her. Angels forbid I should have such thoughts after a day of continual supplication to the Lord.

"I'll sit here." She gestured to a smaller table in the shadow of the portico. A rug and simple pillows adorned it. "Do I need to explain the serving procedure?"

I shook my head and made my voice calm. "This isn't my first feast, madam."

She sniffed again.

I took a breath and plunged into the treacherous storm of her disapproval. "Where will Yeshua of Nazareth be seated?"

"Why does he matter?" The disdain in her tone made fire roar to life in my gut.

Why does He matter? I blinked at her. Because He healed your husband and raised my brother from the dead. Because He is the Lord's Anointed.

"He is also an honored guest." My voice lowered, and I heard the steely tone I often used with my siblings. I gulped. *Yahweh, help.* "My brother would be dead if the Master had not called him forth."

Her chin ducked slowly. "I suppose you are right." She pointed to the seat at the opposite end of the table from Simon. It wasn't considered a position of honor but of service. I clenched my teeth.

The greatest of these is the servant of all, Yeshua's voice echoed in my mind.

Of course, He saw himself as a servant, and He wouldn't be offended by the seating arrangement. Why should I be offended on His behalf?

Forgive me.

Would I be able to go a minute without needing His forgiveness this day?

Back in the cool room, I dropped my shawl, then sat in the kitchen with the cook. We shared the imperfect tidbits. The tender, tasty mutton melted around the warm unleavened bread.

I popped one of the fig tarts into my mouth. Its sweetness delighted my tongue. "You've outdone yourself."

She smiled, sampling one of the crumbling treats. There were more of her desserts than I thought normal, but she wouldn't hear me complaining. Two other serving girls shuffled through the delivery gate. We would have plenty of help tonight.

When Simon strolled through the courtyard dressed in his best robes, I knew it was time for the feast to begin. I washed my hands and pulled the first course from the oven. The roasted roots and herbs filled the heated air with savory goodness, and I was glad I'd already eaten.

We loaded up trays, and I instructed the girls on the serving order. They followed me as I served Laz first and then Simon before working my way around the right side of the table.

Yeshua glanced up at me. When our eyes connected, I felt that same sense of knowledge I'd gotten the day we met.

His mouth gentled into a slight smile, and I slid the plate in front of Him, lowering my eyes.

"Good evening, Master."

"Shalom, Martha. Thank you."

His words, quiet for my ears only, soothed the stress building in my mind. Tonight would be fine. Everything would turn out as G-d intended.

Once I finished serving the men, I went to the mistress, pausing until she motioned for me to set the plate in front of her. Several notable women sat at the table with her, but I didn't see my sister. A folded napkin waited at the low end of the table, so I set a plate there, nodding for the other servers to do the same with their dishes and the wine.

We delivered cloth-wrapped bread to be shared between guests, and I made certain to hand one to Simon so he could recite the traditional blessing. I bustled back to the kitchen to prepare the mutton for the next course. So far, things were going better than I'd imagined.

As soon as I stepped into the dining courtyard with the main course, I smelled the incense.

My sister was spending Grandmother's precious nard on Messiah. Once she broke the box, that was the end of it, and she would not be perfumed on her wedding day.

Sadness tugged at my heart. Mary deserved the best for her wedding.

And Messiah? What does He deserve?

My footsteps slowed, and my stomach tightened. It wasn't that Yeshua didn't deserve the honor because He deserved this and so much more. But it wasn't customary to shower the lowest guest with such anointing if the guest of honor and host hadn't been given similar treatment.

The woodsy aroma of the ointment drowned the rich scent of the roasted mutton and spices. I glanced toward Yeshua as I served Simon.

My sister stood beside the Master, rubbing the fragrant oil into his hair. By the time I reached his place, she'd knelt and began anointing his feet.

"Why was this ointment not sold for three hundred pence?[1]" The scathing tone of Judas Iscariot's voice twisted a knife in my heart.

Oh, Mary. What have you done?

"What a waste!" another man muttered at the same moment Judas said something about the poor.

Yeshua touched Mary's shoulder.

"Let her alone."

His voice held the same gentle rebuke he'd used with me those months ago when I'd singled my sister out for scorn. I served the meat, and his voice flowed over me, not hurting the way it had then. His lesson was designed for someone else this time.

"She has wrought a good work on me. Ye have the poor with you always[2]."

I stepped beside the mistress. She glared at my sister, and I knew her disapproval had nothing to do with the precious ointment. Mary's actions weren't part of her plan.

"Mutton?" I drew Deborah's attention to me and inwardly cringed at the anger etching her features.

Her lips curled down even more before she huffed and

waved at her half-empty plate. I served her before quickly moving to serve the other women.

"Why is she making such a show?" one of the women whispered, and then she glanced up at me. The glittering in her eyes told me it hadn't been an accident, although she covered her mouth as if it was.

"She is come beforehand to anoint my body to the burying,[3]" Yeshua said.

His words didn't register because I was fighting back my indignation at the cruelty of these women.

Yahweh, I am so weak.

I wanted to dump the meat I'd slaved to prepare into the woman's lap. How dare she belittle my sister's sacrifice!

Was it so different when you demanded she help you rather than worship Messiah?

My irritation deflated. No, I hadn't been much different than these women.

Yahweh, help me show them how to honor You.

My hand trembled only a little as I finished serving the whispering women.

Mary was prostrate, using her shiny mahogany locks to smooth the perfume into Yeshua's feet. The men had returned to eating, but those nearest her still frowned toward my sister's horizontal form.

Yeshua wrapped his mutton in a round of bread, and as He lifted it to his lips, our eyes met again. His dark haze held an array of deep emotion: sorrow, pride, and love. Always He loved us, no matter how much we misunderstood.

I ducked my chin and hurried back to the kitchen, wondering at the tears blurring my vision.

Even now, the aroma of my sister's worship fills our small home. By using her hair to minister to the Lord, she retained much of the perfume for herself. How long will it cling to her, reminding her—and me—of the gift she gave to the Lord?

And the gift He gave in return: His approval.

How I wish I had reacted differently so I could have earned that, too.

MY TWENTY-FOURTH SPRING

*J*startled awake. Today was Pesach. I shrugged my robe over my sleeping tunic, eager to see Yeshua before he headed to Jerusalem. Once again, He'd turned down my Seder invitation.

I pushed back the linen curtain and hurried across to the fireplace. Laz and three others were awake and reclining on cushions near the table. I glanced their way, noting Yeshua wasn't among them.

After splashing some water on my face and washing my hands, I approached my brother. "Thank you for the water."

Laz nodded. Most men would see it as women's work, but my brother had been humbled by years as an invalid. Now he was so grateful for the ability to carry the weight of water that he blatantly disregarded customs. Most mornings, he wouldn't need to fetch the precious liquid, but with the disciples present, this would only be the first trip to the well.

As I beat together the flour, salt, and oil for bread, I asked, "Yeshua?"

"Praying," the one called Levi, a tax collector until he'd been called by the Master, answered.

I was outside flipping the dough on our baking stone when Yeshua returned. The sons of Zebedee and Jonas followed him.

Peter sniffed. "Breakfast? We do have time for that."

Andrew nudged past his brother. "Would you like me to carry the finished bread inside?"

I nodded and handed him the linen scarf that contained ten loaves. "Cheese is on the table."

I'd purchased the soft goat cheese from the marketplace, knowing it was the Lord's favorite.

Andrew ducked his head. "We appreciate your care of us."

I reached to pull my shawl over my head, only then realizing that I'd been in such a hurry, I was outside without it. My grandmother would have scolded me for the indiscretion.

"Master." I stood from my squat, gently shaking my knees to rid them of tingles.

Yeshua paused beside me, squatting down so I could return to work. I turned the dough on the stone and balled up more batter. I looked into his face, only a span from mine.

Bags pulled the skin beneath his eyes like He hadn't slept. His compassionate gaze held a darkness, a sorrow, worse than I'd noticed at my brother's graveside. My heart stumbled inside my chest.

"I wish you'd reconsider about Seder. Lazarus says the chief priests are angry with you."

"My time is now. I must eat Passover with the twelve." His quiet voice vibrated with that special something that had drawn me to him from the beginning.

"You know best." *Did I truly believe it?*

"Things will be different now."

I thought he meant because of Laz's fame. Things already were different, but I didn't think they were better. Not that I'd say anything to him about that. I didn't want to sound ungrateful.

Am I ungrateful? I let the question hang in the air for Yahweh to answer as He would.

"You've honored our house by staying here." My throat thickened.

His lips curved into a slight smile, tugging at his beard, but the sadness deepened in his eyes. "You've honored me with your friendship."

"Master—" I planned to thank him for raising and healing Laz, but my voice stopped working. I plunged into the understanding depths of his eyes and knew at once this was it.

Goodbye.

The bustle of fourteen men kept me from having another moment to speak with Yeshua. Mary joined me at the fire, and we quickly finished the baking. Conversation rolled around the room, but before I could even slather cheese on the warm bread, Yeshua rose.

"I'm walking with him to the city," Laz told me. "I'll be back."

I would have given anything to be a man at that moment, to walk out with Yeshua. But I was only an unmarried woman whose entire world had tilted because her disabled brother had died and rose again to his place as head of the family.

As the men filed out leaving the room in disarray, Mary blinked back tears. I stood behind her, inhaling the fragrant incense clinging to her hair and shift, subtle but still potent. With my hands on her shoulders, I leaned into her back, as Grandmother had done with me so many times.

"I know." Those were the only words I had.

How could I comfort my younger sister? The man we loved walked out to face a crowd of powerful enemies. He said things were going to be different, but how?

If you believe, all things are possible. Yeshua's voice echoed through my heart and mind.

Mary sniffled. I pressed my palms into the top of her shoulders, letting the pressure warm and soothe. We stood that way for many minutes.

"I didn't get to say goodbye." Sorrow roughened her musical voice.

Finally, I stepped away from her, grabbed a broom from the corner of the room, and handed it to her. Our gazes locked. Her amber-flecked eyes were luminous pools of regret and loss.

Life goes on. I tried to convey the message with my look. She took the broom and dropped her gaze to the floor.

We went about our daily chores. She left for Avi's before me, planning to weave with the girls for an hour before it was time to begin preparations for the feast. I worked until my lower back ached from the scrubbing, but our little home sparkled.

Laz came just as I pulled my veil out of our storage chest. I would be appropriately attired during the dinner. It wasn't the first time Avi had invited the three of us to share Seder with his family, but it was the first time he had told me I was a guest and should plan accordingly.

A guest? The man was my most generous employer. How could I sit at his table like I belonged?

Laz's face pinched with worry.

"I'm going to the market. Don't get caught up in your scrolls and lose track of time."

Laz tugged me to a standstill. "I'll go with you. I can read at Avi's."

I shook my head. "Any excuse to put your nose in a scroll."

"The smell of ink delights me."

My silly little brother. Maybe I should stop thinking of him that way. He was adapting well to his role as a provider for Mary and me. Even though we'd put off the latest round of suitors, I knew he wouldn't have to worry about Mary much longer. A host of new men from the Weavers' Guild had asked about his younger sister.

I tried not to think about leaving Bethany and the only home I'd ever known. But if he accepted a place with the weavers, the possibility we would move to Jerusalem was great.

Laz carried three scrolls and a quill, and we walked side-by-side through the narrow streets. Rather than taking the small alley to the back entrance of Avi's home, Laz marched up to the front gate and pulled the bell rope.

The house boy opened the door and gave us a warm smile. Laz followed the boy toward Avi's study, but I turned toward the kitchen. I heard Mary and the girls singing from the open courtyard where they weaved on warm, clear days.

Imma rolled balls of dough along a sturdy sideboard opposite the brick oven.

"There you are." She covered the dough with a cloth. "I almost went without you."

"Sorry. I wanted to clean our place."

"The high day throws everything off."

I didn't bother to mention it was the detritus from fourteen men that threw my home into disarray.

We'd been to the market together many times and divided the list and coins between us. Before long, we were back, but she shooed me out of the kitchen.

"Guests don't cook." Her wrinkled face pressed into a smile.

The girls had retired to their room where Mary was brushing Hannah's hair. I offered to do Rebecca's hair but had hardly run the brush through it twice when Avi appeared at their door.

"Father." The three girls stood, although the youngest had to throw off a blanket to do it. I hoped she wasn't getting a fever.

Lord, protect her.

Avi waved his hand at them. "Girls, go back to what you're doing. I need to speak to Martha."

"Miss Martha?" The girl whose long hair I still held turned to gaze at me with wide eyes.

"I hope I'm not in trouble." I winked at her.

The two older girls laughed, but the youngest blinked owlishly. "She's not in trouble, Abba. She's been good."

Avi rubbed his palm over Rachel's cheek. "Yes, she's been good. Just like my three girls."

His gentle touch reminded me of Abba. It had been so long since anyone had touched me with such tenderness. My cheeks flushed slightly at the thought of his palm on my face.

I smiled reassuringly and handed the brush to Rebecca before following Avi out. His steady pace led me down the hallway and into his office, a place I cleaned only when he worked in the temple. But those times were past.

Laz had told me Avi had requested to end his service at fifty years of age because there was no one to care for his daughters. As a successful scribe, he wouldn't face any financial hardship without his portions from the daily sacrifices, but wouldn't he miss ministering before G-d?

When we entered the room, Laz stood. It was such a formal gesture, I stumbled at the doorway. What was going on? The smile on my brother's face should have eased my anxiety, but instead, my heart threw itself against my ribs.

"Avi has—"

"Would you come in?" Avi cut off my brother's words. His warm fingers touched my arm, guiding me toward a plush cushion meant for clients who waited while he worked on their documents. "Sit."

Fire bloomed on my face. Tingles raced beneath his

fingers and up my arm like I was a maiden meeting a suitor. I might be a maiden but one who was too old and tired to dream of suitors.

I sat. Avi poured wine[1] into a brass goblet and handed it to me. I stared up at him before shooting a hot look at my brother. What was going on?

Half of Laz's mouth curved upward. It was a mischievous grin I hadn't seen in many years. My brother raised his eyebrows and looked to Avi.

"I've retired from the priesthood."

I started at Avi's voice, nearly sloshing the drink on myself.

He cleared his throat. "I'm not a young man, but I have discussed this with Lazarus, and he thinks you would be amenable."

His words faded, almost as if he was embarrassed by them. I stiffened. What was my brother getting me into now?

"I only have the highest regard for your family." Sweat beaded on Avi's forehead. Was he nervous? It certainly wasn't hot in the room, although the flush on my face still hadn't cooled.

I glared at Laz. "Out with it," I demanded of him.

He stared at Avi who gave a slight shrug of his shoulders.

My brother leaned toward me and in a fake whisper said, "Avi would like to marry you."

My heart dove, and my stomach bucked upward, creating a collision at the base of my lungs. My fingers tightened on the goblet.

"Your daughters will marry soon." I wanted to ask why he

wanted another wife when his girls were mostly raised.

He blinked. "I am nearly old enough to be your father, yes."

I shook my head. That's not what I meant. He was an honorable man, but he didn't need a wife. The son he lost would have been a priest, but since I wasn't from the tribe of Levi, our son wouldn't.

Our son. But this wasn't about what I wanted.

I stiffened. "You feel sorry for me."

Avi stood. "No. I—"

Laz grabbed my goblet and set it on the table, nearly sloshing the red drink. He jumped to his feet and yanked me up with him.

"He's going to teach me to be a scribe. A scribe!" His face flushed with joy. "Can you imagine?"

I blinked away the rush of hot tears, trying to look beyond my brother and see Avi's expression. I wanted to be Avi's wife. And Laz wanted to be a scribe more than anything. This way, we wouldn't have to move to Jerusalem, and perhaps the unwelcome suitors would leave Mary alone.

I should say yes. Only a foolish woman—once she was an old maid like me—would turn down such an offer. Especially when she'd given up on being married.

But suddenly, I couldn't imagine being pitied every day for the rest of this honorable man's life. We'd been friends—as much as a man and woman could be. He'd been generous and respectful, but I didn't want to be a charity case forever. Even if it meant Laz would get to be a scribe. I had given up enough of my life for my siblings, hadn't I?

I straightened my shoulders. "So, I should marry Avi to get you what you want?"

Laz's mouth dropped open, and then he snapped it shut. "You should marry him because you love him."

I gasped. My face flamed so hot I thought it might catch my veil afire.

Avi nudged Lazarus aside, and my gaze riveted to his face. His brown eyes begged for understanding, and his gentle lips parted several times before he finally spoke.

"I would have offered for you years ago, but I had my duties at the temple." He cleared his throat. The warmth of his gaze melted my resolve. "You and your sister have been more than mothers to my girls."

"I was your late wife's caregiver."

He nodded. "And she's the one who told me I'd be a fool not to marry you."

I gasped, and my knees buckled. I would have fallen except his hands tightened on my shoulders. Lazarus stood behind me, one hand on my lower back.

"Out of pity." A tear burned its way down the side of my face. "Is that really the marriage you want?"

"Stop it, Martha." Laz's voice rose, and it shook me. He never raised his voice in anger. "You're the only person in the room who thinks you're unlovable."

The shame flooding me changed to fury, and I gripped my skirt to keep from slapping him. How dare he raise his voice to me after all I'd done for him? How dare he talk openly of feelings I wanted to stay hidden?

"Please consider it." Avi stepped back, and a shadow fell

over his endearing face. **Oh, Lord, I hurt him.** "Lazarus has the writ."

If he didn't pity me, what was this about? And I'd never said I was unlovable. I just wasn't young and pretty like Mary. If no one had offered for me in ten years, why would things be different now?

I took a deep breath and slapped at the moisture on my face. "Why then?"

Avi sighed. "I'm too old to promise you sons, Martha. But I can give you companionship and a home." He swallowed, and his voice lowered to a gravelly whisper. "And my heart."

His heart? Mine skipped around in my fluttering stomach. Did he truly mean that?

Only believe. Yeshua's words from the day we met outside Laz's tomb echoed through my mind.

"I would rather have your heart than a dozen sons." I hadn't meant to say the words aloud.

Avi's beard parted, and his white teeth glowed like a harvest moon at midnight.

"We'll marry then." He glanced at my brother. "As soon as the rabbi will allow it."

My legs gave out, and Laz helped me back to the pillow. I apologized to him with my eyes, and he smiled so widely I knew he'd forgiven my poor behavior.

I'm getting married soon. Before the feast of first fruits.

Yahweh, it is so much more than I ever imagined. Thank you.

13

MY TWENTY-FOURTH SPRING

*H*ow swiftly those delighted feelings ended, and the stunned disbelief returned. This time it had nothing to do with me or my family, and everything to do with Yeshua. Our Messiah dead?

Yahweh, how can this be Your plan?

I stared into the stricken faces of Andrew bar Jonas and Philip of Bethsaida. Laz nodded somberly as they spoke of Yeshua's demise. Our eyes met across the table. Thankfully, Mary was with Avi's girls. She wouldn't be able to bear this news.

"Crucified?" I still couldn't believe it.

Messiah was dead? G-d's Anointed came to redeem us all, but instead He'd become the victim of a Roman cross?

Andrew's dull eyes swept toward me, and our gazes connected for an instant.

"John bar Zebedee was at the cross with the women and had to hold up the Lord's mother." Philip scowled. "I should have gone, but I ran at the first sign of danger."

"We all did." Andrew squeezed Philip's shoulder.

They made an incongruous pair: the burly fisherman with wild hair and the sleek scholarly scribe with his trimmed beard and fine robes. I was surprised to learn they had known each other since childhood when Philip's family emigrated from the Grecian provinces after his father's death.

Philip shrugged off the work-worn hand. It was the most animated I'd ever seen him. Around our table, he often took notes or made calculations during discussions. His pale brown eyes reflected the disbelief careening through my chest.

"I should have gone." Laz glanced toward his clenched hands on the table.

I couldn't stand his misery. "I'm sorry."

After all, I was the one who discouraged it when the messenger came telling us Yeshua had been arrested and taken to the Roman governor. I couldn't comprehend that an innocent man would be tried and sentenced so quickly. And executed?

I scurried around the table to rest my hands on my brother's shoulders. "The crowd was mad. And I didn't want Mary to go."

After a long pause, Laz squeezed my hand. His palms had the calluses of a scribe, and he would finally earn money while doing what he loved. With the feast and the additional high sabbath, he still hadn't made it into Jerusalem to inform the guild of his changed plans.

"I couldn't have stood there and done nothing." Andrew's voice shook with deep emotion. Not anger or bitterness, but perhaps a combination of both. "Peter disappeared after the arrest, and I expected him to be there. But John told us he was the only one."

"What does it mean?" Laz straightened. "We can blame ourselves for failing Yeshua, but He's never failed us. What does this death mean?"

Movement stirred the skin over our doorway. Avi pulled it aside and paused. "May I enter?"

"Enter and be blessed," Laz said.

The men rose as the older man stepped over the threshold. Stew bubbled in my gut, and my cheeks were fire-touched. My betrothed carried several scrolls in a bag that bumped his hip with each step.

"Wine?" I sidled away from Lazarus. My hands trembled, needing a task.

"Well-watered, thank you." His thin lips tilted, and the look in his eyes held a promise I couldn't comprehend.

I scuttled to serve him as the apostles shared the news of the crucifixion. He thanked me, and I returned to the preparation counter to mix dough for fresh bread.

"It means the sacrifice is made." Authority resonated through Avi's words. "Here. I have Isaiah's prophecy."

The parchment rustled. My hands stalled in their measuring.

Could it be true? Was there a prophecy about Messiah as

a sacrifice? Would we have to wait until the resurrection to see Yeshua again?

He that believes in me though he were dead, yet shall he live. Yeshua's words from the day he called my brother back from Paradise overlaid what the men in the room said. He could raise Lazarus, but who would raise Yeshua?

"Yet it pleased the LORD to bruise him; he hath put *him* to grief: when thou shalt make his soul an offering for sin, he shall see *his* seed, he shall prolong *his* days, and the pleasure of the LORD shall prosper in his hand[1]." Avi's voice made the scripture ring with life and truth.

"Smitten of G-d[2]." Lazarus breathed the words like a prayer.

"Bruised for our iniquities?" Andrew sounded dismayed.

I turned from my work. My heart lurched in my chest. Could this be true? Was Yeshua offering his own soul for our sins? My sins?

But why?

Philip stood and paced, hardly able to take four steps in the room cluttered with pillows. "He's been doing the work of the Father. Why would He forsake Him this way?"

"Let me read." Avi cleared his throat. "He shall see the travail of his soul, *and* shall be satisfied: by his knowledge shall my righteous servant justify many; for he shall bear their iniquities[3]." Avi stopped, and his face glowed with a holy discovery. "The Passover Lamb in actuality. Don't you see?"

The other three gaped at him.

The hollow of my stomach ached, and I pressed my hand to it. Oh, to hope that this death served such a great purpose.

And why not? Yeshua's life was lived to help others, should we have expected his death to be different?

"This is not all. I had word from my brothers at the temple." Avi glanced around at the other men.

"What word?" Philip rejoined them around the table.

"During that earthquake yesterday afternoon, the veil between the Holy Place and the Most Holy Place ripped." Avi pressed his hands flat on the table. "From top to bottom."

His voice shook with unbridled joy. Joy! He wasn't insensitive to our grief as we discussed the death of the One we loved, but he couldn't contain his emotions. Amazement, awe, and joy bubbled from him.

"Don't you see what it means?" Avi glanced between the three men.

"Impossible! That curtain is too thick." Philip crossed his arms.

"From top to bottom?" Laz's eyebrows dipped together.

My brother was losing his grief-stricken expression. This was making sense to him.

"Earthquake. Darkness. Acts of G-d." Andrew panted the words.

Avi met the fisherman's gaze. "Yes. The G-d of Abraham, Isaac, and Jacob ripped the veil that divides the temple on Earth from the mercy seat in Heaven."

We gaped at him, but something buried deep in my soul sang.

"The price for mankind's sin was paid. The innocent sacrificed for the guilty." If anyone knew about the shedding of innocent blood, it was a priest. "My righteous servant—Yeshua—shall justify many[4]. That's what happened!"

Avi clapped his hands. As if a dozen incense burners flared to life, a sense of worship filled the room. Isaiah's words echoed and rebounded while the men continued to question Avi.

Yahweh, is this true? Even as I prayed the question, the peace I'd felt the first time I looked into Yeshua's eyes engulfed me.

Yes, it seemed to say, *Yeshua has finally finished his work.*

"That's wonderful!" The words escaped before I could draw them back.

Laz blinked at me. Slowly, his lips relaxed and turned upward. "Of course. He can't claim His earthly kingdom until He settles His heavenly one."

"But he's gone." Andrew voiced the unanswerable.

"Am I gone?" Laz leaned forward. "I died, but now I'm alive. Our Heavenly Father will do the same for Yeshua."

Like a trumpet blast, the words pealed throughout the room. Laz proved that death didn't stop Yeshua. If Yeshua could raise my brother with Yahweh's power, then Yahweh's power could raise Yeshua.

A smile came from the deepest part of my soul. "Yes."

The men looked at me. Avi's eyes filled with a pride I never expected to see from anyone. Laz nodded his chin once with final firmness.

"Yeshua will rise." My brother looked to my betrothed. "When?"

Avi fingered the parchment. "Let's search the scriptures and find out."

Praise G-d for Avi.

While I made bread and put together a simple meal, Avi distributed his scrolls, and the men began to pore over them.

Hope fueled us all.

14

MY TWENTY-FOURTH SPRING

*E*arly on the first day of the week, I carried a pot of water past a pair of women on their way to the city well, and we exchanged greetings. The simple words didn't stop my mind from whirling through the schedule of daily chores. When I stepped into our yard, I was still compiling the list for the marketplace.

Mary flew out the door of our house, collided with my chest, and sent me stumbling backward. Her arms circled my waist as she steadied me, and water from the jug on my head sprinkled us with a refreshing mist.

I hadn't seen her face glow like this since the evening of Simon's feast.

"He's alive!" The scent of sleep clung to her breathy words.

I lowered the water jug to the ground and scooped out a bowlful, dumping it into one of the jars beside the wall.

"What are you talking about?" I cocked my head toward the jar that stayed on the table beside our bed.

"Yeshua." Her eyes sparkled brighter as she said his name.

Yeshua was alive?

My hands finished filling the jar for the kitchen, but the lists I'd been compiling during my walk disintegrated. Yeshua was alive?

Mary bounced on her toes, beaming brighter than the rising sun.

Of course he was! We'd been expecting to hear it, hadn't we? Ever since Avi, Andrew, Philip, and Lazarus searched Avi's scrolls for the prophecy of Messiah's death and resurrection, we had wondered when his return would happen.

My heart floated like an airborne feather, and my head spun a little.

"Tell me everything." I nudged our jar closer to her feet with my toe. "As we work."

"How can you work?" Mary balled her fists on my fluttering sleeves. "I want to shout and sing and dance."

"I can work because my stomach wants to eat." I smiled to take the sting out of my comment. "But I also want to hear everything."

"Yeshua's alive." Her wide eyes stared into mine.

I nodded. "How do you know, Mary? Was he here?"

Her smile fell away, and my heart plummeted with it. I shouldn't have assumed he would come to our house. He probably appeared to the apostles first. We might not ever see him again.

My empty stomach twisted. *Until Paradise.*

Because I *would* see Him in the afterlife.

Mary grunted as she hefted the jar. I followed her into the house. Laz poked the coals of the fire in the hearth.

"Yeshua lives." My brother's smile transformed his haggard face. "Just as the scriptures foretold. Avi is a wise man."

Indeed. Avi's wisdom had stayed our grief, and that was an honorable use of heavenly wisdom.

Thank you, Lord, for such a man.

My heart did a strange two-step flutter at the thought. Is this what being married would be like? I would feel odd at every thought of Avi?

Mary bustled through the curtain to our room and returned empty-handed. I set my jar on the counter and began to mix dough for our daily bread.

"The women and Jesus' own mother went to the tomb before daybreak." Words spilled from my sister's lips.

The day had fully broken in the last fifteen minutes as I returned from the well. How early had these women gone to the tomb if word had already reached us?

"You just missed the boy they sent." Laz poured wine into a jug and topped it off with water.

"Heavenly messengers at the tomb rolled the stone away." Mary's voice pitched in a way that reminded me of the little girl she no longer was.

Heavenly messengers? What a sight. What a fright. A shiver tingled up my spine.

"No one mentioned the guards." Laz sipped from a

goblet, looking pensive. That suited his face more than the smile he'd flashed moments earlier.

"Stop." I held up my hands, one toward each of my siblings. "Who read the message?"

"Heard it." Laz said. "Andrew sent a fleet boy with the news."

I glared at my brother. "This doesn't make sense. Mary, tell me about the women."

Laz opened his mouth to argue, and I hardened my expression. He closed his mouth and gestured toward our sister.

Mary clasped her hands together. "A group of women took Yeshua's mother to the tomb so she could anoint the body. She never got to say goodbye."

None of us had. Yeshua's solemn look from the morning of Pesach flashed in my mind. Sometimes words weren't needed.

I returned to my flour, sprinkling it with salt and oil.

"Messengers in white were at the tomb. One sat on the stone, and one sat where the body used to be inside." Her voice thickened.

"He is not here," Lazarus muttered. A ripple of emotion churned along the back of my neck. "He is risen, as he said[1]." His eyes met mine. "I never heard him say that, did you?"

I shook my head. "He told the apostles everything, though. And his aunt and cousins traveled everywhere with him. They must have heard."

Mary shifted closer and laid her hand on Laz's head. Her

nimble fingers burrowed in his shoulder-length locks. "She said I was supposed to tell it."

Laz started, and his face flushed. All our lives, that would have been a sign of a fever. These days my brother could suffer embarrassment with the rest of us and not cause me a bit of worry. My lips twitched toward a smile.

"Thinking out loud." He squeezed Mary's hand.

Her lips softened, reminding me of Mother's soul-deep rare beauty.

"So, what happened then?"

"The women ran to Zebedee's family home in Jerusalem to tell the disciples. Many were gathered there. Peter and John ran to the tomb, and Andrew sent the messenger to us."

"After breakfast, I'm going to Jerusalem." Laz's announcement made me blink.

"I want to go with you." Mary stared at me, eyes wide and pleading.

My empty stomach lurched toward my throat. Why did they need to go? We could wait together for more news.

I rolled the dough into balls. "Finish the bread. I'll make a cheese spread."

I felt their eyes boring into my back as I shuffled out of the room, wiping flour on the underside of my shawl. I crawled behind Laz's bed and jerked up the door to the cool space. Only a small dish of the soft cheese remained, but I took it up anyway. Something else to add to my market list.

When I returned to the main room, my siblings stopped their conversation. I hadn't heard a thing over the creak of the boards and sliding of furniture.

"I will watch over Mary." Lazarus straightened in his seat. "We can send a message to Avi's once we learn more. I suppose you'll be there."

"After I deliver notice to my other customers." I crushed some turmeric and bay leaf into the soft cheese, pressing it together with a pestle.

Mary knelt beside the hearth, turning loaves on the baking stone. My empty stomach filled with flutters. I should have kept her there, protected her. But she was grown, and she loved Yeshua as much as the rest of us. What responsibilities did she have that I couldn't cover?

"Let's see if Avi will send his boy with you. That will save time in searching out a messenger." As I spoke, Laz stared at me, mouth opening slightly.

My sister brought the fresh bread to the table, her eyes lowered. After reciting the blessing, we ate in silence. When we finished, Mary stood to clear our cups. I stilled her hand.

"Get ready. I'm eager for news."

Her eyes flared with joy. She flung her arms around my shoulders and whispered, "Thank you" again and again in my ear.

"We'll be fine." Lazarus rose to his full height beside me.

I nodded. Something lodged in my throat so I couldn't speak.

They were grown up, and it was time for me to let them go their own way.

Yahweh, go before them. Keep them safe.

The second prayer was almost an afterthought. *Thank you for raising Yeshua.*

~

As THE MORNING dragged its way to noon, I worked on. When the boy arrived, the message he carried didn't share much more news than we'd learned that morning.

It was nearly nightfall, and Avi dropped my shawl over my shoulders. His warm hands rested on my upper arms.

"I will walk you home." He stepped closer. "Next week, the rabbi will hear our vows."

My heart and stomach danced wildly. Yeshua's death had dampened my joy, but with this news of an empty tomb, it had returned in greater magnitude. Sometimes, I wondered if I might float away like a cloud.

A knock sounded on the gate, and then my brother and sister traipsed through the courtyard. I rushed forward, nearly leaving my shawl in my betrothed's hands.

"What news?"

"I spoke to Him. To Yeshua." Lazarus glowed with purpose. "He wants me to encourage other believers in Bethany."

I shook my head. Laz's being alive and healed constantly spoke encouragement to believers in our town. What did that have to do with Yeshua?

I stepped past him. My questioning look met with only a small smile from my sister. She shook her head, all the fervor and delight from the morning gone from her face and eyes.

"I didn't see him. I was at the market with Mary Magdalene. Her story..." A sadness glinted in my sister's eyes. She hadn't spoken with Yeshua, but something had happened, something that dimmed the hope she'd had that morning.

"I want to hear everything." Avi gestured toward the cushions against the interior wall. "I'll walk Martha home afterward."

"I'm going to check on the girls." Mary shuffled away, head down.

My heart went with her, but I wanted to hear my brother's news.

Yeshua lived. He'd appeared to my brother to give him a future purpose. Would he visit me as well? And what happened with Mary?

I learned that as we prepared for bed.

"He comforted Mary Magdalene in the garden by the tomb," Mary said.

The way she stumbled over the other Mary's name nagged at me, but in the excitement of Yeshua's appearances, I didn't analyze it.

"So, he's appearing to everyone?"

My sister shrugged. "I didn't see him." After a long pause during which the sound of the brush stroking her hair mingled with our breathing, she said, "Mary loves him too."

I opened my mouth to say, *We all love Yeshua.*

"Not that way. Like a woman loves a man." *Like I love him.* I knew my sister's heart. "And he chose to comfort her."

I laid the brush aside and pulled my sister close. She rested her cheek on my shoulder, but no tears fell.

"He is not meant to marry. Not to Mary of Magdala nor to you."

"But a king must have sons."

I shook my head, stroking her waist-length dark hair to soothe the bitterness of this truth. "He has a heavenly kingdom. It's about eternal life, not defeating Rome. That's what we learned from scripture."

"Why, Mary? Why not me?" The woe transformed her into a creature of melancholy. My Mary dreamed big dreams and sang her way through hard days. This girl—no, woman—was a stranger with sad eyes and a woe-filled voice.

Yahweh, give me words to help her.

The crunch of bristles smoothing her silky hair filled the silence. I let the rhythmic motions soothe her as they always calmed me.

"Men line up to marry you, sister. You are comely and desirable, but Yeshua is not meant for one woman. He loves all of us in a bigger and deeper way."

Help her understand. Show her this truth.

My fingers stroked her silky hair, and the action centered me. Would she refuse to marry? She had to marry. She deserved a family more than any of us.

"The way he made me feel."

I massaged her scalp underneath the heavy curtain of hair. She sighed, and some of the tension in her neck and shoulders melted.

"God's love makes all of us feel that way," I murmured into the side of her face. "It will be different with the right man. Special."

She pulled back and blinked at me. "Like how you feel about Avi?"

Heat flushed my cheeks, and I withdrew slightly. "Like I will love him when we are man and wife."

And for once, I believed the truth I offered my sister, one that could give hope and not just pain.

Yahweh, send the right man for my sister. Show her how a man's love is different from Yours. From Yeshua's.

None of the men in Bethany were right for her. Neither were the men from the Weavers' Guild. None were men who would cherish my sister the way Abba cherished Mother.

Maybe no one could love us as truly as Yeshua, but I believed there was a man who could mend the hurt in Mary's heart.

Show us this man, Yahweh. Help me trust Your plan.

15

MY TWENTY-FOURTH SPRING

*I*t had been twelve days since Laz saw Yeshua near the garden tomb. Although Mary and I hadn't seen him, He had appeared to his apostles several times. Mary was more upset about this than me.

Mostly because I couldn't think of anything except: *Today, I'm getting married.*

I might have been old for a first bride, nearly twenty-five summers, but Avi had looked beyond my plain face, work-hardened hands, and stubborn personality. My mother taught me a good wife wasn't supposed to be bossy, but I had to be in order to survive since Abba died.

Show me how to be a good wife to Avi. Even if it means taming my urge to speak my mind.

A wrestling match waged in my stomach. After I finished the final knots of the blanket I'd woven for Avi, I folded it carefully and wrapped it in a length of linen purchased last week. I planned to fashion that fabric into a tunic for my husband very soon.

My husband.

I sucked in air.

"Come bathe," Mary called from the doorway of Laz's bedroom.

Soon, my brother would have the house to himself, since Avi agreed Mary should live in the nanny's room at his home and continue teaching his daughters. Although the older two attended the synagogue school, his youngest had another year before she'd reach the required age. Avi was certain that Mary would be married before then.

Lord G-d, make it true.

But neither Laz nor I would force her to choose someone.

Several neighbors helped us move Laz's bed out of the room so the tub and a makeshift dressing area could be erected in our parents' bedroom. Avi provided me with a white tunic for the ceremony, and Mary and Imma worked feverishly to complete a bridal veil.

My stomach cramped again. I thought of the virginal white wool lying on the mattress in the room across the hall. That's where the *chuppah*[1] would occur in a few hours.

At the thought of consummating the marriage, I clutched my stomach. Mary bustled across our small home and hugged my arm.

"Nervous?" Her eyes smiled while her lips pursed.

"I might vomit."

She jumped back, and I scowled at her, but her antics eased the ache in my middle.

"You should save that for when you're expecting." The twinkle in her eyes nearly blinded me.

I shook my head, not even noticing the sharp pang in my heart. "Avi's too old for that."

Her eyes widened. If it was anyone else, I would blush, but it was Mary. I was the one who had to explain where babies came from, and why she was bleeding when she began her monthly cycle two years ago.

"He told you that?" She covered her mouth with her hands.

I shook my head and disrobed. I caught sight of the fine, white linen tunic, similar to what priests wore to minister at the temple, hanging on the dressing screen. My breath tried to choke me.

The robe's simple lines were meant to be adorned by a colorful sash and the intricate edging of a veil. A fish symbol embroidered on the front of the skirt in golden thread declared our faith in Yeshua as Messiah.

I wished He could attend, but I didn't know where He was. If the reports from Andrew and Philip were accurate, Yeshua was back in Galilee, but if rumors were true, He'd been appearing to apostles in Judea, too.

I sank into the water. Warmth seeped through me and relaxed the knots in my center.

Mary stared at me, and I remembered we were in the middle of a conversation.

"He apologized when he asked me to marry him." I looked down to rub olive oil into my arms. "He already has children."

"But not a son." Mary's voice was low.

She spoke from behind me, and a moment later, warm water streamed over my hair. I sighed at the pleasure of her fingers rubbing oil into my scalp. The flowery scent of narcissus perfumed everything as she massaged from my forehead to the top of my ears and down to my neck.

I relaxed into the wooden basin. When I washed my hair, I used tepid water and was always rushed, so her ministrations were another special part of this remarkable day.

We both scrubbed at my wet flesh until I was clean. I stood, and water sloshed around my calves. Mary kneaded jasmine-scented oil into my back. The specialty blend was expensive, but Lazarus insisted I have it. "You only get married once," he'd said.

Until a few weeks ago, I never thought I'd get married at all.

Yahweh, thank you for this blessing. I don't deserve it.

With G-d, all things are possible. I knew Yeshua had preached this many times. I'd heard my brother repeat it, too. He believed it, and he should know since he'd been to the world of the dead and come back to the land of the living.

I believe you, Yahweh. You can do anything. Even give a child to an old man.

A son.

But it seemed too selfish to pray for such a thing. God had already given me more than I ever imagined.

Before long, I was dressed, and the sun dipped toward the horizon.

Imma arrived with a beautiful pair of sandals. Her brother-in-law was a cobbler, so I knew he gave her a bargain, but she was not a wealthy woman. Braided leather in three shades of brown ran across the top of my feet, and the soles were thicker than anything I'd ever worn.

"They're beautiful." I hugged her.

She smiled, but a tear rolled down her face, tracing the wrinkles that showed her accumulated years.

"For a lovely bride. May Yahweh bless your home and make it fruitful."

Laz held out a lovely red sash, so dark it's nearly purple. Threads of gold were woven through it. I gasped as he wrapped it around my waist. After he tied it, I fingered the loose ends, and in the fading sunlight, the gold winked and sparkled.

"This is incredible." Tears blurred my vision. I was too happy for weeping, so I blinked them away.

"For my incredible sister." Laz and Mary stood in front of me. "You've sacrificed so much for us, and we're happy that you're finally getting something you want."

I hugged him, surprised how wiry and strong he felt in my arms.

Another blessing from you, Yahweh. One we never expected. Thank you.

When I hugged Mary, she brushed her lips against my cheek. "My older sister is getting married. Now Yahweh will send a husband for me."

I stared at her. She was serious. Had she been refusing suitors these past two years because she wanted me to get married first? I hoped not. We were both ready for husbands to love.

Distant trumpets sounded. My attention swept to the door. Through the opening, the ringing of timbrels and singing voices mingled.

My bridegroom was coming for me.

He arrived with the rabbi. We spoke the traditional confirmation words of our covenant. Then the rabbi shooed my family and Avi's outside.

I heard Mary start a song as I turned toward my bedroom. My stomach knotted again, but I led my husband to the room. Once I'd proven I was virtuous, the true celebration could begin.

AFTER OUR NOISY processional through Bethany's five streets, the growing crowd ushered me into the courtyard of Avi's home. Even though I'd been there hundreds of times, today felt different.

Our home.

Guests bustled around Mary and me, their singing boisterous still. I clutched Mary's hand. She'd skipped beside me in the streets, and I could hear joy in every word she sang. Her twirls reminded me of my final summer of childhood before the plague that changed us all.

Things were changing again for us.

My empty stomach ached and dipped. My sister's fingers caressed mine as if they were Laz's feverish brow.

Yahweh, help me be the wife Avi needs.

Avi waited beside the door to the inner dining room. Servants I didn't recognize carried tables into the courtyard, too, but Mary pushed me toward my husband.

I blushed at the thought of everything that had happened today and ducked my head as Avi and I were seated at a small table facing two longer ones. Friends and family—men at the table to our right, women and children on the left—reclined on cushions.

Wine flowed. Avi raised his cup.

"To a godly wife and a blessed house."

The crowd repeated his words.

Avi turned to offer me the first sip from his cup. I reached for the bottom of my veil and lifted it far enough so my lips could taste the liquid. I'd hid behind the thick fabric earlier as we'd hurriedly consummated our contract. My throat thickened, so I tried not to think of my embarrassment, or I would choke on the spicy drink.

After my sip, Avi drank and put the cup down. His ink-stained fingers reached for the veil, and he turned it back, so the folds of fabric hung over my hair, which was braided and twined in a rope that hung between my shoulder blades.

"Thank you." My cheeks burned. There'd be no more hiding now.

Avi smiled. One of the guests raised a cup and called out, "To a fruitful union."

Every cup raised and voices repeated the common wedding blessing. My heart raced, but I knew better than to hope.

Servants brought the feast to our table first. Between courses, I glanced at the guests. Mary was sandwiched between Avi's daughters. At the head of that table, Simon's wife picked at her food. She looked up, and our gazes clashed. She didn't smile, just blinked before frowning at her plate.

Of course, Deborah wasn't happy with the delectable *kubbeh*[2] or the leek soup. I knew Simon and Avi shared many interests, so I would likely be entertaining the woman in the future.

As an equal.

The laughter and talking voices faded away. I blinked and stared at the bowl of soup Avi and I shared. With thick, savory broth and chunks of vegetables and meat, it was delicious, better than anything I'd ever eaten. My chest and stomach tumbled together.

Should I feel nervous about rising to a different social status? This change wouldn't make Deborah like me because I was the same person I'd always been.

Slippers shushed on the stone floor behind me, bringing the room back into focus. A hand hovered beside the bowl. I nodded, and the woman whisked it away. A few moments later, a bowl filled with warm bread settled between Avi and me.

"Are you well?" His voice was mild, and he leaned close, so a whisper of his warm breath grazed my chin.

I peered into Avi's eyes. He—my husband—stared intently into my face, wearing the same worried expression he'd had when I first came to the house to care for his mother.

I dipped my chin, keeping my eyes on his. The festive

atmosphere faded again, and this time my heart pulsed into my neck.

In a few hours, we would be alone in our home. The back of my neck burned, and a sudden itch screamed for attention on my scalp.

"Let me serve you the bread." My voice sounded airy, like Mary when she'd run all the way home from the well with exciting news.

"Thank you." His beard twitched. "I prefer dates over raisins."

I escaped from his mesmerizing gaze. My hands were steady as I smeared goat cheese on the bread. I sprinkled a couple of dates over the cheese and folded the bread. I held it toward his mouth.

My stomach danced again. He glanced from the food to my eyes and never looked away while I fed him. In a way, this action seemed more intimate than the consummation we'd performed at my childhood home an hour ago.

"More raisins for me." I sounded breathless again, and a blush flooded my face.

Avi chewed the bite and then chuckled. "You're going to keep me young, Martha."

Keep him young?

The twinkle in his eyes made me forget about the wrinkles around them. If he looked at me that way every day, life would be better than I'd dared to dream.

16

MY TWENTY-FIFTH SUMMER

*S*everal days before Shavu'ot,[1] we headed to the capital. Yeshua's disciples had passed the word that the followers of Yeshua should meet together this first day of the week. They'd invited everyone to the upper room in the home of Mary Mark, and I tried to imagine how the crowds who followed Yeshua would fit into one room.

Avi and Laz walked in front, heads bent together. Laz was seeking Avi's advice about ministering to infirm believers in Bethany, what my brother sensed was the heart of Yeshua's final instructions to him. Laz had already spoken with Simon Peter about it, but many details regarding the Lord's vision for his assembly of followers needed to be worked out.

I squeezed my sister's arm, but she didn't look up. The biggest story the disciples had repeated was about clouds taking Yeshua back to Heaven, and Mary had grown quieter since then. She had hoped to see him again, but now it wouldn't happen until we saw him in the afterlife.

To some people, this sounded crazy, but since I had watched Yeshua call my brother from the grave as if Laz was simply in another room, nothing the Lord had done surprised me anymore. He could do anything because He was as much G-d as Yahweh.

For weeks, Avi had been talking about Yeshua being Yahweh, but my mind couldn't grasp that. G-d lived in Heaven, but Yeshua lived on Earth in a body much like mine. How could such a thing be if He was the G-d of Abraham?

Now that Yeshua was also in Heaven, would it be easier to accept this doctrine?

Finally, the familiar dusty road met the city's cobblestones. People bustled through the streets, and we were just a small cluster among many.

The Mark family lived in a sprawling building with two courtyards. Andrew told us we were gathering this First Day in a room where Yeshua and the apostles had eaten and slept on several occasions, most notably for the final Seder.

Although we arrived many minutes before the appointed time, the outer courtyard teemed with people. Men gathered on the stairs to the upper room, pressing tightly to the wall of the house so we could pass.

Upstairs, several couches and pillows were shoved to the center of the room, and all other furnishings had been removed. The air was close with the scent of too many bodies. I wished for an open rooftop and noticed another set of stairs led to that space.

Large windows on two opposing walls had been uncovered. Light and air wafted through but not enough to keep the heat from rising. If everyone came inside, we would roast like birds over a fire.

A woman old enough to be my mother sat on cushions in the center of the vast room. I didn't recognize her, but John bar Zebedee attended to her. Three other young men surrounded her and a younger woman, who touched the head of a baby the older woman cradled with reverence.

Laz immediately pulled away from us and approached the group. I leaned against the back wall, pulling Mary next to me. Avi settled beside us.

"Perhaps you should take a seat while you can." He motioned toward the cushions.

"I think the old and infirm should have the first chance." I didn't bother to glance toward Laz or the group of hearty individuals he'd gone to converse with, but my meaning was clear.

Avi pressed his lips tightly enough for his facial hair to appear conjoined. "That is the Lord's mother and brethren."

My heart plunged into my stomach.

Oh, Yeshua, I'm sorry. I didn't mean to speak poorly of your family.

Behold my mother and my brethren. I heard the echo of His voice and pictured him motioning to everyone in the packed room.

We are all family now. That's what Yeshua taught. Still, I couldn't believe how easily condemning remarks flowed from my mouth about His family—*my* family. And on the First Day in a service to honor his resurrection! After all, the woman I'd maligned had been chosen by G-d to give birth to His son.

Yahweh, forgive me. Teach me to hold my tongue.

I'd been humbled for the moment, and that was proof I could change my bad habits.

Your mercy is great, oh Lord.

A few moments later, Laz and one of Yeshua's brothers worked their way through the growing crowd. I watched the man whose hair and beard were cropped shorter than normal, in a style many laborers wore. His eyes were browner than Yeshua's, and his face had a certain rugged quality that made it eye-catching.

He's more handsome than Yeshua.

The thought brought heat to my stomach. I shouldn't be noticing that about another man. I glanced sideways at Avi and dropped my gaze. He watched the duo approach, too.

"These are my sisters." Laz halted in front of us, and the carpenter of Nazareth stopped beside him. "Martha, wife of Avi and Mary."

The stranger's brown eyes widened, and he looked confused for a moment. He nodded toward me.

"I am James bar Joseph, carpenter of Capernaum."

"Capernaum? But Yeshua was from Nazareth." The words burst out of me.

What was that I'd prayed about controlling my mouth?

Lord, forgive me. I can learn.

James' full lips quirked. Laz shook his head, but I could tell he wasn't embarrassed.

"Indeed. My older brother, Judah"—he motioned toward the man still seated beside his mother— "runs the shop there. I started another in Capernaum, where I make orders specifically for the merchant family my sister, Abigail, married into."

I nodded, pursing my lips to keep from spewing other unwelcome words. Avi pressed a hand into my back, soothing me with his gentle presence.

G-d, thank you for this man You gave me.

"Avi bar Thomas, Levite and scribe."

The men pressed their forearms together and leaned in to touch cheeks. My heart warmed to see Avi so close with our Lord's brother.

We are all his brethren.

It would take a while to assimilate this idea. I was so accustomed to being the big sister, responsible for every weight of the family. But no more. I was responsible for my husband's daughters and household, but the concerns of my siblings were shared by my spouse.

Shouldn't that make me feel lighter? Instead, I felt flustered and unprepared.

Lord, help me.

James turned a warm gaze on my sister. "Mary." He swallowed, and his tone grew a touch husky. "I have asked your brother's permission to court you. Will you grant it, as well?"

Mary's chin lifted, and she looked at him for the first time. Color seeped into her cheeks behind the thin veil she wore. I knew my sister well enough to guess she was noticing his handsome features just as I had.

I bit the inside of my cheek. As silence stretched, I elbowed her gently in the ribs.

"Why?" Her quiet question was nearly lost in the jostling press of people.

James shuffled closer and leaned forward to whisper in the ear closest to me, but he was still far enough away that he didn't touch either me or Mary.

"Yeshua said the sister of his friend Lazarus of Bethany was to be my bride."

A strange shudder rippled through me. It began in my ear where his words touched something, then raced down my neck, arms, torso, and legs. Finally, even my toes tingled.

Yeshua had not forgotten us. He might not have appeared in his resurrected body to me or my sister, but He made provision for important things pertaining to our futures.

Yeshua, thank you for taking care of my concern for Mary.

I stared at my sister. Her face flushed a deeper shade of pink, and light flared in the lovely brown pools of her eyes, igniting the quartz flecks that sparkled in sunlight.

"Did my brother give permission?" The familiar melodious lilt was back in her voice.

Lazarus glared. "I would never disobey Yeshua."

My lips twitched into a smile at his indignation. He'd disobeyed me often enough as he was growing up. Our gazes met, and he widened his eyes and pursed his lips. Now was not the time to tease him about it.

I'm learning, Yahweh. I am.

"Indeed. But I wouldn't do anything against your will." James drew back, and I admired his earnest honesty.

Although he didn't look much like Yeshua, clothes and haircut aside, his gentle manner reminded me of the Lord.

Moisture burned the back of my eyes. Having the Lord's brother as the husband of my sister would almost be like having Yeshua with us again.

I am with you always. I hadn't heard him speak the words, but when Andrew repeated them to me, I'd known it was true.

Thanks be to Yeshua who keeps his promises.

Simon Peter moved to the front of the crowd and held up his hands. "Let's get settled, so I can call this assembly to order."

"Yes." Mary's answer was firm.

James smiled, and he became even more handsome. He nodded. "I'm sitting with my mother, but I wish to speak with you after the meeting."

"Yes," Mary whispered. Moisture sparkled on her thick eyelashes.

I hugged her to my side. My heart sang with the joy I saw in her gaze.

Thank you, Yahweh. You didn't have to provide such a perfect answer for my sister, but I am so grateful you did.

Avi's arm pressed into my side as we leaned against the wall. The shuffle of feet replaced the chatter of voices, and the noise level dropped away. The crowd stood shoulder to shoulder in the large chamber.

"Let's pray." Peter raised his hands toward Heaven.

His words rumbled over me, but I don't recall them now. I do recall that I worshiped the One G-d of Abraham, Isaac, and Jacob in the Name of His Only Son, Yeshua.

Praise Yahweh for innumerable blessings.

By the grace of Yeshua, I will learn to serve Him—Them—with humility and determination, not stubbornness, pride, or duty. By the grace of Messiah.

So be it.

Amen.

Martha often is held up as an example of what not to be like. This has often grated against me, and the more I study the Bible, the more I realize that many "non-examples" have been misunderstood by theologians and laymen.

I believe Martha of Bethany falls into this category.

If you've finished reading this book, I hope you see that Martha was just a woman whose responsibilities weighed her down. Jesus Christ knew this about her, and He loved her anyway, because it's in His character to love unconditionally.

Did you get that? She wasn't perfect, but Jesus loved her in the midst of her imperfections. Often, we think, *I'm so glad Jesus loves me in spite of my imperfections.* But I'm beginning to believe He doesn't even notice them. He looks at us and sees who we will become once we've sold out to His will. This broken, scarred, faulty person we are in the moment will become so much more.

By the Grace that Jesus extends.

As you reflect on Martha's family and life, I hope you'll remember that Jesus loves you. Jesus loves you and me like he did this trio in Bethany.

Write a brief description of Lazarus, Martha, and Mary. How did your conception of them change because of this story?

Chapters One and Two

What is Martha like at the beginning of the story? Why is she this way?

What is Lazarus thinking about at the beginning of the story? Why do you think this was so?

What impression do you get of Mary? Think of your own siblings (if you have any) and consider how your impression of them might be different from what other people see and think.

How does Martha's impression of her siblings change the story? Or does it?

What do you think of the way they met Jesus?

Do you think it's unrealistic to paint Lazarus as not seeking physical healing? Why or why not?

Chapter Three

This chapter is pure fiction, but I believe it could have happened this way.

Think back to when you first accepted Jesus Christ as your savior. What changed the most for you? What things in life were easy to change? What things were hard to change?

We all face diverse struggles, and God has an answer for all of them. Unfortunately, when people judge us, it makes it difficult to keep moving forward.

What difficulties did Martha face?

How does reading about them in "her words" help you face your struggles?

Chapter Four

Read Luke 10:38-42.

I've heard this preached and taught as if Martha is going about things all wrong and every woman on the planet should strive to be like Mary. But the more I read and study it, the more I think that's *not* the correct interpretation.

What does Jesus *say* that makes people think He's condemning Martha?

How do you think Martha is feeling in this passage? Why does she feel that way?

Have you ever felt like that?

**Author's note: I've heard women at a church function claim to be a "Mary." One woman says it while there is a ton of work to be done—let's say setting up, serving, or cleaning up a meal for a crowd. She says, "I'm a Mary" as she sits beside another woman chatting about life (and not in a way that's ministering to another who is unable to help) while the work circulates around them.

I've been a cranky Martha who demanded everyone help before. It's not any more honoring to the Lord than sitting around in order to avoid the work while claiming you're worshiping or ministering. Remember, we can only be responsible for our actions and attitudes, so try not to judge others.

What's the "one thing" Martha missed that Mary chose in this scene?

**Author's note: I'm not positive that what I used in the story is really the *one thing* Jesus meant. I think the reference is vague enough that the Spirit can teach us about our *one thing* using this passage.

How can you choose wisely but still be true to your personality?

**Author's note: Martha is not the kind who can sit idly by while there's work to be done. But she doesn't use serving as an excuse not to learn about Jesus, love Him, or worship Him either.

Check your heart to see if you can say the same in the midst of your busyness.

Chapter Five

What is a day in Martha's life like?
Read John 11:1-2.

We don't really know the circumstances around Lazarus' sickness and death. In the setting I imagined, I connected every aspect about the Martha we see in scripture. First of all, Martha appears to be the oldest child, but she wasn't supposed to be the head of this household. However, a plague —poliomyelitis was common in that era as a summer plague in large cities, so I used it because I knew a man who had survived polio and had a withered arm and one leg shorter than the other—had crippled him. I wanted to give Lazarus a reason for not being in charge of his sisters, since it's clear from scripture that he wasn't.

Have you ever ministered to a sick family member?

How do you feel when they get worse, no matter what you do?

Do you go to God first? Or is sending a note to Jesus a last resort?

**Author's note: In hindsight, we know Lazarus' death led to a greater purpose, but his sister's do not know this. They only know the sole protector in the patriarchal society where they lived was sick and dying.

How does your perspective affect the way you pray?

Chapter Six

I've lost a sibling. He died suddenly when he was eighteen. None of us expected it. I've also sat at the bedside of a sick loved one and watched them breathe their final breath. I don't recommend it.

Consider the losses Martha has suffered. How is she feeling?

Do her feelings change once she learns Jesus is coming?

Have you ever felt resentment toward God? Like He showed up "too late" to help you through a hard situation?

I have. It's not a sinful feeling. But it can lead to bitterness if you *stay* in that state. Give those feelings to God. He can handle your anger and resentment, but He can't forgive you if you don't ask Him to do it. When those negative feelings take root, that's when "normal" things slip toward "sinful."

What do you learn from this portrayal of Martha's meeting with Christ?

How can those things help you the next time you face a difficult situation?

Chapters Seven and Eight

Read John 11:17-45.

Did reading the events from Martha's perspective change anything about how you've read this story in the past? If so, what?

Contrast the reactions of Mary and Martha. Which do you think you would be more like in this scene?

I've always marveled at Martha's directness. "Lord, he stinks." As if she's telling the Creator of the universe something he doesn't already know. What surprises you most about Martha in this scene?

How do you think Jesus is feeling at this event? How do you think his disciples feel? The crowd of people gathering?

I've been to too many funerals in my life, but it's still hard to imagine what it would be like if the dead person stood up during the service, fully alive and fully healed.

What do you think it would feel like to see a loved one resurrected at their funeral?

Does imagining it strengthen your faith in God?

Everyone Jesus healed was immediately and completely healed. I believe that power would translate to restoring a dead body to perfect health. What did you think about Lazarus' total healing?

Chapter Nine

What does Martha struggle with after Lazarus is healed?

**Author's Note: The Bible doesn't say Lazarus was crippled before he died or healed afterward, but this is one area where all my "why" and "what if" questions couldn't see another reason for Martha to be in charge of their household. Even if she was older (unless he was *much* younger), he would still be the head of the house.

Do you think Martha's struggles are realistic?

How do circumstances make you ungrateful at times?

Martha didn't pray for help until after she'd already tried to fix things. Do you ever wait to pray?

Recall a time when you did this, and when you finally prayed, God worked things out in short order. Thank Him for hearing and answering prayer.

Chapter Ten

This recounts the feast at Simon's house. I made him one of Martha's clients because I couldn't think of a reason she would be asked to serve (unless they were related). However, I wanted to keep some conflict in her life, and having a Pharisee's wife looking down on her seemed to fit.

What was the purpose of the spikenard *before* Mary used it on Jesus? Did Martha agree with Mary's decision to anoint the Lord?

Why was Deborah antagonizing Martha? Do you have people in your life who always seem to be trying to "get your goat"?

Say a prayer for any that come to mind. How might you show them the love of Christ the next time they are frustrating you?

Why do you think Deborah didn't approve of this feast? Does she believe Jesus is Messiah?

Have you ever wished you'd reacted a different way in the aftermath of an event? What is the best way to deal with these feelings?

Chapter Eleven

Passover is an important Jewish feast. Most Jews in the first century traveled to Jerusalem because men were required to sacrifice at the temple. I had my cast observe this feast at Avi's house (not in Jerusalem) because Bethany is close enough (less than two miles away) that the men would be able to make their sacrifice in the morning and still return for Seder in the evening.

What do you think of Martha as an older sister to the much younger and quite different Mary?

If you have siblings (I do), you know that your differences can cause joy and arguments. How do you think Mary felt about Martha's form of comfort? Was she comforted?

How important is it for us to customize our comfort (or exhortation or encouragement) to the recipient? Is this something you are good at? Or do you need more grace to minister to others?

Martha feels uncomfortable being a "guest" in a home where she's used to being a servant. Have you ever felt like this? How does it affect your response to your host/hostess?

Martha is shocked by Avi's proposal. She had given up hope that she would ever marry, and the idea of being married out of pity—even to a man she loves—appalls her. Have you ever mistaken someone's intentions? How did that work out?

Are you quick to apologize when you realize your error?

Do you thank God for his unexpected blessings in the moment or as an afterthought?

Write a few predictions for Martha's future. We know what's about to happen to Jesus. How do you think that will affect what she's feeling? Her relationship with Avi?

Take a moment to reflect on the blessings God showered on you today. Thank Him for them. Praise Him for them.

Sometimes, it's good to be like Martha.

Chapters Twelve and Thirteen

Then came the dark days.

Try to imagine what it felt like for the disciples to see the hope for their future perish at the hands of their oppressive government. As much as it is my gift to imagine things, this was difficult for me to do.

How do you think you would have reacted to the death of Jesus? Who in the story do you relate to the most during this dark time?

**Author's Note: I've always wondered why the disciples didn't look to the Old Testament for answers when Jesus died. Then I realized they didn't have access to it the same way we do today. But Avi, as a priest and scribe, did have access. In fact, if he copied Isaiah over and over for his job, he might have had the fifty-third chapter memorized.

Read Isaiah 53. What did you think of Avi's response to the apostles' grief?

In Chapter Thirteen, Martha makes a big change. What is it? Why do you think she changed in this way?

What do you think of Martha's attempts to comfort Mary at the end of the chapter? Did she say the right things? How could she have handled it differently?

God tells us that He "comforts us in all our tribulation, that we may be able to comfort them which are in any trouble" (2 Corinthians 1:4). How is this true for Martha in this situation?

What are some difficult things you have faced? How might you use what you learned to help others who are facing similar struggles?

Chapters Fourteen and Fifteen

Jewish weddings are huge celebrations that involve several days of feasting. Because Martha didn't have a long betrothal period, I gave her a shorter wedding, too. Men in first-century Jewish culture commonly took a second (or third) wife if their first died.

What sorts of thoughts plagued Martha on her wedding day? If you're married, what sort of things did you worry about on your wedding day? How are the thoughts similar or different?

What did you think of Mary's and Lazarus' gifts and gestures to Martha? Did it change the way you saw them?

Weddings in first-century Israel were much different than even Jewish wedding ceremonies today. My research made me a little uncomfortable. What did you think of the consummation ceremony? Why do you think things were handled in this manner?

How would you describe Avi's and Martha's marriage? Do you think it was typical or atypical for that time (and even today)?

What makes a "good" marriage?

What did you think of the church service in the last chapter? How is it similar to and/or different from what we do today?

**Author's note: I debated ending this story at a different place because this ending gives some of Mary's story away. Still, the plan had always been to end at the same church service as in *A Pondering Heart*.

Did this fictionalized account expand your insight into these familiar Bible stories? Did it help you understand Martha in a new way?

How can reading this and other fictionalizations help you understand Bible characters?

How does understanding Bible characters help you grow in your Christian walk?

Thank you for reading *A Laboring Hand*. If you have any comments to share, I'd love to hear them. My email is info@sharonleehughson.com. I have a special folder called "fan mail" that I *love* adding to when I hear from readers.

I hope I'll see you in Bethany again for *An Adoring Spirit*. No matter how much you think you know all about her, Mary's story still holds some surprises.

Blessings,
Sharon Hughson
Author

Aids for Group Study

Martha of Bethany has a lot to teach modern-day women. Part of the joy of writing biblical fictionalization comes from knowing a story based in scripture can speak to every part of a reader. My biggest hope is that it makes the Bible and its stories come alive in new ways in the heart, mind, and spirit of every reader.

Sometimes, the best way to grow spiritually is to discuss the Bible with other believers. Aiding that is the purpose of this section. Here I'll outline a few ways you could use this book in a small group setting.

Ideally, this would be a women's Bible study, but this book wasn't written with the idea of excluding male readers. The first book in the series, *A Pondering Heart*, was read and reviewed by a few men, and they seemed to enjoy the story.

A BOOK CLUB READ

Although I designed the Reflection Section to aid in personal growth, it could be used to guide a book club session.

Depending on your group (most book clubs meet once per month and discuss a different book each time), you could determine how to read and discuss this book. However, all book clubs expect members to read the text outside of the meeting times.

In this case, it would be essential for the leader to read the Reflection Section and decide which questions the group would discuss at their monthly meeting. Check out the Topical Studies section below if you'd like help deciding on specific topics to discuss.

Is your group reading for pleasure? If that's the case, you might want to focus on what made this story an enjoyable read. If your members are familiar with the Bible stories surrounding this, they probably have different thoughts than those who are unfamiliar with Lazarus, Martha, and Mary of Bethany.

Is your group reading this for spiritual growth? If so, you'll want to focus on Chapters Four and Five, or Seven through Nine. These are the chapters that are loosely based around scriptural accounts.

Decide what you want to discuss. How to serve God? Service versus worship? Those topics are central in Chapters Four and Five.

If you're discussing faith or prayer, using Chapters Seven through Nine will open various avenues for you to take those discussions. Perhaps you'll choose to read select portions of John 11 and then ask how the fictionalization portrayed these things. Or maybe discuss how seeing things from Martha's perspective added to the understanding of the scripture.

Be sure to reiterate that *A Laboring Hand* is fiction based on fact. All the emotions and circumstances not directly seen in scripture are creations from the author's mind and heart.

A FOUR-WEEK BIBLE STUDY

This book makes a perfect study guide for a Bible study group. This is how I would teach the book.

It will take four meeting sessions to discuss the book. Perhaps your group meets weekly, bi-weekly, or monthly. Any of those would work.

At the meeting, before you begin the study, make sure every member has a copy of the book. Create a group "portrait" of Mary, Martha, and Lazarus based solely on personal ideas.

MEETING ONE

Before the meeting, every participant should read Chapters One through Five.

At the meeting, read Luke 10:38-42. Choose which of the discussion questions from the Reflection Section you'll discuss. Make sure you prioritize them. It's important that you keep your study to the allotted time frame.

Assign the reading of Chapters Six through Nine for the next session.

MEETING TWO

Before the meeting, decide which verses from John 11, you'll read during the study. Pick out a handful of questions from the Reflection Section to discuss alongside the verses.

Before you begin the meeting, ask the ladies to describe Mary, Martha, and Lazarus and define their relationship with Jesus.

Read the scripture you've selected. Discuss it and the questions.

Before the next meeting, group members will need to read Chapters Ten through Thirteen.

MEETING THREE

For this lesson, the group will read John 12:1-8 and discuss these events as well as the state of mind of the disciples in Chapters Ten through Thirteen.

Pick out the questions from the Reflection Section you'd like to discuss and prioritize them.

I encourage you to take the time to discuss the character of Avi in this session. Why was it Avi who wanted to search the scriptures? How did he offer hope during this dark time?

It's important to understand that every child of God is called to be Avi in our present world. We have the hope of Jesus Christ, and those who don't know him are hopeless (even if they won't admit it or can't see it). Discuss how we can be agents of light in our dark world.

Make sure everyone knows they need to finish reading the book before the next meeting.

MEETING FOUR

Decide what you want to focus on in this lesson. You could focus on the change Martha makes from the beginning to the end of the story. If you do, read Luke 10:38-42 and John 11:20-45.

Choose and prioritize any question from the Reflection Section you'd like to use during this final session.

During the study, make a chart. Use either a white board or a large piece of poster board. Make two columns, and title them *MARTHA BEFORE JESUS* and *MARTHA AFTER JESUS*. You can have each participant come up and add to the columns, or you can lead a discussion where you fill out the columns.

Then point to the Before column and connect it with a trait in the After column. Ask, "Why/how did Jesus change Martha from *before* to *after*? Guide the discussion to bring out the points the Spirit lays on your heart.

If your group would like to correspond with me, I would *love* to hear from them. You could create a single letter that tells me what you learned from this study, or everyone could write their own.

Feel free to email me at info@sharonleehughson.com to ask for a mailing address. I'd love to fill a binder with these missives proving God used this story for His glory.

TOPICAL STUDIES

The story of Martha lends itself to many topical studies. These are a few that stood out for me as I was writing the book.

Worship vs. Service

Although Luke 10:38-42 has often been used to condemn Martha, I'm sure Chapter Four debunks this idea.

Use Chapters Four and Five, as well as Eleven, to teach about these two aspects of our Christian lifestyle.

Think about worship. Characterize it.

Differentiate it from service. Note that service focuses on *others,* while worship focuses on *God.* Our service can be worship when we choose to serve to honor our Lord. However, our worship will become nothing if we lose our focus on Christ.

Discuss the "one thing" that is needful. I had Martha decide it was a right spirit. What other ideas does your group come up with?

Note the differences in worship and service, as seen in Chapter Eleven, while Martha serves food, and Mary washes Jesus' feet. Discuss if Martha was also worshiping when she served Jesus. Appreciate the diversity of opinions on this because there can't be a right answer when none of us know the hearts of these women or the Lord's perception of them.

Loss and Grief

Choose portions of John 11 to read as a group. Decide on a few excerpts from Chapters Six through Nine that you'd like to read and reflect on during your together time.

Death isn't the only loss we face. List other losses.

Do we pray before these happen? How does a loss affect our faith?

What is grief? Talk about the process of grieving. Do you wish our culture was more like what is shown in Chapters Seven and Eight? Why or why not?

How does our society's treatment of grief affect us? Does it honor God?

How can we change the perspective of "they're in Heaven, so why are you crying?" that often permeates Christianity? If it makes sense for your group, you could create a list of pointless and hurtful platitudes offered to a grieving person. Then, change them. What could people say instead that would make a difference?

I would *love* to hear your lists. Please send them to info@sharonleehughson.com.

Praying God's Will and Accepting His Answer

At the end of Chapter Fourteen, Martha prays for Mary's future husband. In the final chapter, we meet this man.

Was this an answer to her prayer she liked? Would it have been different if one of the other suitors became the right choice?

Consider a time you prayed for God's Will and liked the outcome. Why did you like it?

Considering Martha's story, think about how she wanted to ask Jesus to raise Lazarus. When He did, how did she feel? But did those feelings remain in the chapter that followed? Why not?

Sometimes the answer we think we want doesn't turn out the way we expect.

This is why it's important to pray for God's Will rather than our own. Even in cases where the two match, sometimes the way an answered prayer plays out catches us off-guard. We expected it to look or feel different.

Think of a time God's Will in your life was completely unexpected. How did you deal with that?

We should always be thankful for answered prayer, but an attitude of gratitude is something we have to learn to cultivate (1 Thessalonians 5:18).

Finding Hope in Hard Times

Check out Chapter Thirteen. It's not the only one that blooms with hope, but it's the most obvious one for discussion.

Read Isaiah 53. Find all the references to Jesus' crucifixion. Now imagine being alive and seeing the brutal scene. Why did it take Avi to bring the similarities to light for Andrew and Philip?

What are some scriptures that have offered hope to you during dark times?

Prepare to share with your study group. It can be difficult to bare your soul in such a way, but it can also encourage others. Two things are likely to happen:

1. No one will say anything.
2. Others will share similar encouragement from other scriptures.

Whatever the case, allow God to lead the discussion. Don't force the issue.

Growing as a Christian

During first-round revisions of the manuscript, I cut the scene that reveals Martha's ongoing struggles from this manuscript. It just didn't add to the story. But I think the struggle is clear anyway.

Choose some character traits of Martha (and her siblings) and discuss how they changed through the book. Believe me, all three of them changed.

How does this encourage you in your Christian walk? Even though this is fiction, these characters should be an encouragement to you. They are based on real people. I couldn't have imagined the real struggles they faced, but I did imagine some.

What struggles did they face? How did they deal with them? Did they overcome them?

What struggles are you facing? Are you dealing with them? Avoiding them? Ignoring them? Praying about them? Honestly seeking God's help to overcome them?

A final note

What other topics and themes did you find as you read the book? I would love to hear from you. Please send me your thoughts and/or questions to info@sharonleehughson.com.

I have spoken to groups about creating fiction from scripture. If you would like me to come and speak to your group, please contact me through the form on the Author Info page of my website (sharonhughson.com) or send me an email at info@sharonleehughson.com.

In this era of amazing digital technology, I have author friends who have attended book clubs using applications such as Zoom or Skype. I would be willing to do the same if it's possible.

Most of all, thanks for reading this story.

Blessings,
Sharon Hughson
Author

Did you enjoy Martha's story? Did it make you wonder what her sister was thinking?

Turn the page to read an excerpt from **An Adoring Spirit**, the third book in the **Reflections** series.

In it, you'll know exactly what little Mary of Bethany was thinking during Lazarus' illness, at the grave and while she anointed Jesus' feet.

AN EXCERPT FROM AN ADORING HEART

My cheeks blushed with heat, and my veil slid down my braid as I ran home from the center of town. It was really happening! We would get to meet the miracle worker!

I burst into the house. "It's true!" Excitement stole my breath.

Martha turned from chopping at the wooden counter, and her eyes widened at the sight of me. My attention flitted to my brother.

Laz fixed bright eyes on me and asked, "Where?"

I wanted to dance around the room and clap my hands. Instead, I skipped closer as I told him, "At the temple. But the rumor is he'll be returning to Galilee after the Sabbath."

The Sabbath was still a day away. Too long for my brother to wait to see the man he suspected could be The Anointed One. Israel had waited for hundreds of years for the promised Messiah's deliverance. What's one more day?

Laz clutched the scroll spread on the table in front of him. "We must go tomorrow. Stay with Cousin Nathan."

I nodded, eager to make plans.

Martha's voice cut across the joy-filled moment. "What are you two plotting? And you know better than to invite yourself to Nathan's house."

As much as I didn't want to admit it, she was probably right about our cousin. He held a grudge against Martha and Laz for surviving the plague that killed his family so long ago. He spoiled me, though.

"Fine. Avi's family has a place." Avi was a priest and scribe who both Martha and I worked for every week. He was kind to us. Martha said it's because we're orphans, but I liked spending time with his daughters, so I pretended we're all one big happy family.

I sidled closer to Martha. The bread I'd baked while scouting for Laz's information in town warmed my side. "I'm sure we can sleep on their roof."

Martha shook her head as I stepped up and set the bread beside her chopped vegetables.

"I made extra bread for the journey and the Sabbath." I didn't understand why she wasn't as excited about meeting Yeshua of Nazareth as Laz and me.

Without glancing in my direction, she said, "Thank you." She scooped the vegetables into a pot and held it toward me. "Put this on the fire."

I wanted to scowl at her attempt to remove me from the conversation, but excitement bubbled fiercely in my stomach. I snatched the pot and raced toward the doorway. The sooner the soup was cooking, the sooner we could plan our trip to see Messiah.

On my way out the door, I heard my sister ask, "What are you talking about?"

I slowed my steps, but I knew I couldn't turn back. I had to obey Martha.

Father G-d don't let her ruin our plans.

With a charred stick, I stirred the coals on the outdoor fire we used for cooking and cleaning. I added scraps from a small pile of broken branches beneath an overturned pot resting against the brick wall. Flames kindled. I stacked two larger wooden blocks, castaways from the Carpenter's Guild, over the coals before leveraging the cooking triangle into place and fitted the pot atop it.

I skipped back inside. Martha glared at my feet.

How could I forget to remove my sandals? I doubted it really made much difference on the packed dirt floors, but I backtracked to the door. I swallowed my sigh and slipped the shoes off, sliding them beside my sister's. They were practically the same size. The days when I was the little girl had disappeared. Wasn't it time for her to stop treating me like one?

"I can't wait to hear Yeshua teach." I gasped at the next thought. "Do you think he'll heal anyone?" I nodded toward the withered arm hugging my brother's side. "Maybe he'd heal your arm."

Laz shook his head, like I knew he would. "I don't want anything from him. Only to learn if he is the Anointed One. If he is, then I'll follow him."

Martha's hands gripped her womanly hips. "You'll do no such thing."

I don't really remember my mother, but I recalled our grandmother using this posture many times. The pose made my sister seem old and cranky, and because it caught my attention, I almost missed what else she said.

"You can barely walk to the community oven. You aren't following this stranger all over the countryside."

Her attack on him made my eyes water, but it didn't faze Laz.

He returned her glare with unblinking intensity. "Where is your faith, sister?"

She harrumphed and strode outside, forgetting to slide her shoes on.

I smiled at my brother, and he ducked his chin before smiling back.

My mind created an elaborate meeting with Yeshua at the temple. He would be tall and handsome, and he would heal Lazarus, even though my brother would never ask for anything.

With Laz whole, the guild would let us be weavers again. I would be able to weave all day long, making the beautiful patterns I dreamed about. Martha would marry-someone— and stop trying to be my mother. She'd have her own children to mother.

It was one of my favorite dreams.

～

Before the tenth hour on Friday, I knocked on the back gate of Cousin Nathan's home. With Avi's donkey and cart, the short trip from Bethany hadn't taken much time, but Martha grunted like she'd been walking all day.

Liakim answered my knock. At only ten summers old, the boy was nearly as tall as me.

"Mary!" He stepped forward, a smile lighting his dark eyes. Before his lips could agree to his happiness, he said, "Master Nathan isn't expecting you."

Master Nathan? Liakim's mother had nursed Nathan after the poliomyelitis plague took his family. Sarah was like a second mother to him, but my cousin insisted on keeping a strange master-servant hierarchy in place.

"We've come to hear Yeshua of Nazareth." Did I sound as young as Liakim?

"The healer?" I nodded, and Liakim glanced toward Laz. Everyone assumed my brother wanted to be healed.

I didn't understand why Laz didn't want to be healed, but I knew he'd never ask for healing. He only wanted to discover if the miracles meant this man from Galilee was Messiah.

The thrill of meeting him raced up my spine again.

My siblings and I followed Liakim inside. He left us with his mother before returning to care for the animal and cart. I moved to follow him because it wasn't really his responsibility. After all, I was the one who'd asked Avi to lend us the cart.

Martha's hand on my arm stopped me from helping the boy, and we followed Sarah into the main room of Nathan's home. I know Martha still thought of it as Uncle Simeon's home, but I didn't remember him or any of the others who lived here before.

Nathan perched on a stool behind a large loom. The music of threads plucking against the strings tingled through my fingers. He nimbly laced wool with speed and precision, and my hands itched to join him.

"Your cousins from Bethany," Sarah said.

Martha's back stiffened as she edged toward the loom.

Nathan stilled and glanced up with hazel eyes. They narrowed, and I could tell he wasn't happy to see us.

"Cousins. I wasn't expecting company." His tone confirmed his displeasure.

With her spine as straight as any tent pole, Martha said, "Lazarus and Mary are on a mission to hear the Galilean speak."

Our cousin's thick brows rose toward his thinning, gray-specked hair. "Following the rumors of healing, are you?" His lip curled into something of a sneer when he glanced at Laz.

I sidled closer to my brother, who bowed his head in a reverential salute. "No, but I have my reasons."

Martha stepped toward Nathan as he slipped from behind the tool of his trade. A moment later, he greeted Lazarus and finally his cool, dry lips brushed my flushed cheeks.

"Cousin," I said as I returned the greeting.

Nathan huffed out a great breath and swept back to the loom. "Sarah can get you some refreshment."

Martha raised her eyebrows at me, and even before she said anything, I knew what that meant. "Mary will bring it."

She thought she saved me from slaving over the loom with our cousin. I didn't understand that either because I was thrilled to use our father's craft whenever I could. I dutifully followed Sarah into the small kitchen.

The older woman pointed me toward the shelf of goblets while she poured water into a jug of wine. As she worked, she regaled me with Liakam's latest successes at school and with their neighbor's pottery wheel. She hoped he would secure an apprenticeship soon, and I told her I would miss seeing him during visits.

I prayed my children would follow their hearts. If they wanted to work in a field other than their father's, we would encourage them.

My face heated. *We.* The mysterious faceless man who would offer Laz a generous troth for the honor of marrying me. I smiled at my silliness. I had so little to offer a marriage.

Would my tender heart and willingness to bear children be enough? I would honor my husband's household any way I could, of course.

Father G-d bring a man for Martha so I can marry before I'm an old maid.

In a few minutes, I carried the tray bearing an assortment of fruit, the pitcher of drink, and goblets into Nathan's work-room. I offered refreshments to everyone. Nathan took a fig and asked me to pour his wine.

Laz poured his own drink and quickly swallowed half of it. I refilled his goblet before he excused himself and took the cup to his room.

Martha asked after a few people, but Nathan's short

replies didn't encourage conversation. She drained her cup and refused my offer to refill it.

I watched our cousin weave, enjoying the hum of the threads and the shimmer of the pattern emerging as he worked the loom.

"This will be a fine cloth." The pattern in the weave was subtle, so I guessed it was intended for a garment.

"The Tailor's Guild has contracted me for winter cloak-weight cloth."

I opened my mouth to offer to help when Martha cleared her throat.

"I'm exhausted. Mary, help me settle in the room."

My two elders nodded to each other, and I followed on my sister's heels. Her shoulders drooped. She worked too hard at her many jobs, but no one could stop her.

Few words were exchanged before we shared the ink and quill, both penning words in our journals.

Tomorrow, I will meet Yeshua of Nazareth.

Father G-d, is he the Promised One?

The next morning, Laz awoke early. I had to encourage Martha to get up because at our cousin's house she wasn't even responsible for making breakfast. I didn't mind helping out, but today it gladdened me that I wasn't required to fill the water jugs.

Within an hour, the three of us pushed through the crowds surging toward the temple. Many worshipers offered sacrifices or prayed before spending the Sabbath in labor-free pursuits. In Bethany, the synagogue was the most crowded place in town on Sabbath days.

Laz's eyes sparkled as he and Martha broke a path through the narrow streets. Animals bleated and voices muttered in the strange cacophony always present in the capital. Aromatic herbs mingled with overworked animals and unwashed bodies to give me reason for shallow breathe.

I pressed my veil over my nose, and my heart and stomach tumbled together. What would Yeshua be like? Would he be pious like many of the elders? His reputation of healing convinced me he'd be more compassionate than many of the temple workers.

The press of people heading into the outer court slowed us. Once we passed the threshold, a masculine voice carried over the hum of other voices and continual footsteps.

My brother pushed ahead, and I nestled beside Martha, jostling her arm. I peered over her shoulder.

At the center of the crowd, a bearded man sat on an over-turned cart. I sucked in a deep breath. That must be Yeshua of Nazareth, miracle worker.

His amber-flecked brown gaze swept across the circle of faces surrounding him. Unlike the priests, his beard was unkempt, and unadorned brown hair cascaded onto his shoulders. His broad face wasn't handsome, but as his eyes met mine, the world stopped.

Every dream I'd ever dreamed reflected from his wise, solemn eyes. He knew me. He understood me. A trill of recognition sounded in an empty vale inside my chest. This was indeed God's chosen.

"A certain man," he said, and his penetrating gaze swept away as he began a story.

Even though his gaze traveled past me, my heart stayed in that moment of connection. Yeshua of Nazareth wasn't like any other man, and I wanted to soak up every word he spoke.

"Let's get closer," I whispered into my sister's ear. "With Laz."

The press fought our attempts to reach Laz. Martha followed me like a lamb trailing its mother. What was wrong with her? Usually, she would be the one taking charge. Was she upset we'd insisted on meeting Yeshua?

People pushed from the other direction, trying to leave the temple. Others scuttled closer to Yeshua.

Several men with the shaking sickness fell before the teacher. Two younger men supporting a third man staggered to a stop behind the prone men. All of them sought Yeshua's healing touch.

I pushed onto my toes and peered between the crush of bodies. Laz lingered at the outer edge of a group of scribes. One of them asked about the law, and I pressed through a small opening, dragging my sister with me.

"Have you spoken to him?" I asked my brother. The heavy scent of incense in the air barely masked the salty musk of his sweat.

Laz shook his head.

Yeshua answered the scribe with another story. Martha relaxed against my side.

I gazed at the master teacher. His words burned away the irritation of pushing through the crowd after ignoring Nathan's growls about "nothing good coming from Galilee."

My heart yearned for the words of G-d, and today this man with a voice of authority dispelled that emptiness. The spirit of joy and peace that welled inside me whenever I heard the Holy Words rose from deep in my soul.

Messiah has come. Baruch haba baShem Adonai.

Beside me, Martha pressed her veil over her eyes. I glanced in her direction. She wiped tears away, and that made my chest squeeze. She hadn't cried since Grandmother died. Because I was staring at her, I saw the moment her gaze locked with Messiah's and the way her shoulders relaxed and her expression softened in response to him.

I clutched her arm. My gaze collided with Yeshua's again. Assurance flooded through me.

We've found Messiah, and I will follow him to the end of my days.

Martha shook beside me. I wrapped my arm around her waistline.

Praises I couldn't translate into words flowed from my heart and soul. I worshiped the G-d of my fathers. In the Holy Temple, my soul sang a wordless song honoring the unfathomable glory of the Everlasting Father.

Today, at last, G-d had come to deliver Israel. In my heart, everything changed.

To read the rest of Mary of Bethany's story, pick up a copy of **Reflections Book Three, An Adoring Spirit.**

AN EXCERPT FROM A PONDERING HEART

The day my world changed began like every other day in recent memory. An orange sun rose over the brushy hills. Pasty clouds chased each other across the blue expanse of sky. A refreshing chill from the autumn air nipped my cheeks.

I meandered along the worn dirt path. My destination was the same as every morning: the cave beneath the terraced hillside where my father planted his crops. Over the past three years, the path had worn to little more than a rut beneath the constant traffic of my sandal-clad feet and the goats' sharp hooves.

At the mouth of the cave, I swung the wooden gate toward myself and ducked to keep from knocking my forehead on the rocks. Not that I was tall, but the entrance wasn't even six spans[1] high.

When I entered our makeshift stable, the milk nanny rubbed her nose against the wool girdle that secured a water bladder to my hip. I pushed her away, scratching her forehead to ease the rebuke. She whined. One look at her engorged udder explained her urgent desire to follow me out of the pen. With one hand on her leather collar, I secured the gate behind me. Not a moment too soon. The other goats pressed their faces through the wide rungs. Their persistent baas echoed around the cave.

I patted a few of their heads. Pushing the shawl back onto my shoulders, I knelt to begin the task of milking. A hummed tune lifted my heart and kept the bleats of the kids in check. My thoughts wandered to the dream I had about my wedding last night. Rather than my face being hidden, the face of my groom was covered with a veil. Some say dreams have significance. If that's true, what did this one mean?

Soon, the udder hung limply, and the nanny pushed her nose into the enclosure. I never had to tie her as long as her kids were penned up. Most of the young ones were meat goats, not her babies at all, but she seemed to adopt them anyway. The goat knew mothering better than Anna, my father's wife. But I shouldn't complain. It would harden my spirit, and if my stepmother had taught me anything, it was that I didn't want to become bitter.

I carried the pot of milk through a narrow tunnel into a cool room. Light filtered through several fissures. I strained my eyes to make out the large pot and small jar sitting on a ledge in the wall. I placed the fresh milk beside the other containers and reached into the large pot.

The sour smell of curdling milk stung my nose. The curds were still too small and soft. At least one more day before the cheese would be ready for draining. One less thing on my list of responsibilities for today. I sighed. I loved making the cheese almost as much as eating it, but I hated listening to Anna complain about the smell when I brought it into the house to mix in the herbs and salt.

I scuttled back to the main cave, wiping my hands along my skirt. The goats bleated as I opened their enclosure. My little flock surrounded me, snuffling at my girdle, hoping for a treat. I laughed, fondling their ears while leading them into the scraggly grass surrounding our home. Now that the harvest was well past and Father's winter wheat plucked its head in the midfields, foraging became a chore. There wasn't much fodder, since they had been grazing these fields for a month. The time for selling the young ones neared. Luckily, the market for goat meat never waned in Nazareth.

With a critical gaze, I studied the three male kids. I would need to choose the most perfect one and keep it for Pesach[2], still four months away. Since I had begun caring for the goats, Father always let me decide which one was unblemished and fit for sacrifice.

Gamboling, frolicking, nipping at each other, the kids led the way to the watering hole. Adults pulled chunks of grass, wayward leaves on the bushes, and even strips of bark along the way. All around me, the pasture looked forlorn. It was nearly time to stake my herd closer to the house, where they would clean up the remainder of Anna's vegetable patch. Of course, I would need to be doubly certain she was finished with it. For such a small woman, her rants stung like a whip. At least she saved most of them for me or my sister, Mary (how confusing to have two Marys in the house), leaving my not-quite eight-year-old brother Jesse unscathed.

The sun rose, and my breath no longer misted in the cool air. I glanced at the sky, measuring the height of the sun. Still plenty of time to sweep the floors before Anna trekked to market, leaving me in charge of the young ones and preparing the midday meal for Father.

I herded the goats back into the cave, promising to give them another chance to graze before dinner. Maybe I was crazy for talking to them. They weren't human after all. But life could be lonely on a farm.

I pulled the jar of fresh milk from the cool room. Amazing how a single hour in the dark space dropped the temperature. I carried it in the crook of my elbow.

When I left the cave, a draft pushed the scents of goat, manure, and moldering straw away from me. I didn't mind the smell of the goats, but fresh morning air always relaxed me. My shoulders sagged, and I trudged away from the cliffs, never too anxious to return to Anna's domain.

As I rounded the bend, I glanced up at the dusty track leading to the house. What I saw froze me in place.

A most unusual man blocked the path. His white flowing robe reflected the sunlight. Golden-white hair haloed his sharp, pale features, which sparkled with iridescence. Eyes the color of the sky, seeming illumined from within, pierced me as easily as a sharp knife.

"Hail, thou that art highly favored."[3] His voice shook the ground. Or maybe that was just my legs trembling.

My heart thumped against my ribs, and my breath

gurgled in my throat. I clenched the pot, unwilling to let my morning's work fall prey to my terror.

"The Lord is with thee," the man continued. "Blessed art thou among women."[4]

My mind spun, waking, at the strange greeting, from the paralysis his musical voice caused. How was a farmer's daughter highly favored? Certainly the dung caking the soles of my sandals sang a different tune. Who was this man to assure me of my relationship with Jehovah? Yes, I prayed each morning and night, as Father had taught us all, but how could this one know that?

Most disturbing was the final part of his greeting. Only one woman would be considered blessed among the daughters of Eve and Sarah. I was not that woman. I was just a girl.

"Fear not, Mary." He extended a pale hand toward me. "For thou hast found favor with God."[5]

Was this a heavenly messenger? I loved Jehovah as much as any of my friends, but why would the Almighty give honor to a girl like me? A haze of unreality veiled my mind.

"And, behold, thou shalt conceive in thy womb, and bring forth a son, and shalt call his name Jesus."[6]

Now I knew the messenger had the wrong house. I couldn't have a baby, because I didn't have a husband. Yet. Was he accusing me of being intimate with a man? My face flushed.

"He shall be great, and shall be called the Son of the Highest: and the Lord God shall give unto him the throne of his father David."[7] I admit I gasped at this. "And he shall reign over the house of Jacob for ever; and of his kingdom there shall be no end."[8]

My stomach dropped to my feet, and my arm lost all strength, sending the clay pot plummeting to the earth. It splattered near my toes, sloshing goat's milk onto the barren ground. The words proclaimed by this messenger echoed the prophecies of old and the promises made to my father's great-grandfather. The phrasing matched words spoken by my father's deep, warm voice during our evening devotions. A similar thrill evoked by those recitations tingled along my skin.

This messenger spoke of the Messiah, but what he said couldn't be true. I could prove it to him.

"How shall this be?" When I asked about this delicate subject, heat flooded my face, and I couldn't look directly at the man. "Seeing I know not a man?"[9]

I was betrothed, yes, but I remained innocent. I might be a simple farm girl, but I knew how children were planted in a woman by the man's seed. And I had never been with any man in the intimate way reserved for married couples.

I pictured the kind face of my betrothed, and my heart skipped in my chest. He was godly, handsome even, but we had never even touched hands. To lie with him as a married woman? I couldn't imagine it.

The Lord's messenger didn't seem surprised by my question. He continued without pause.

"The Holy Ghost shall come upon thee, and the power of the Highest shall overshadow thee."[10]

A verse Father shared from the prophet Isaiah rang in my

mind: "Therefore the Lord himself shall give you a sign; behold a virgin shall conceive, and bear a son, and shall call his name Immanuel."[11]

My mouth dried like summer-parched ground. I forced saliva in, swallowing past the pomegranate in my throat.

"Immanuel?" It still came out as a whisper.

The angel-I can hardly believe Jehovah sent an angel to me-nodded and said, "That holy thing which shall be born of thee shall be called the Son of God."[12]

My mind, whirling and bucking, refused to process the full meaning of these words. Even as I'm jotting the whole thing down now, it seems so unreal. A fantastic dream.

"Thy cousin, Elisabeth, she hath also conceived a son in her old age," the man in white said. "This is the sixth month with her, who was called barren."[13]

Elisabeth? She had been an old woman when last I saw her. Older than Father. Women that old were beyond child-bearing years.

The angel gave a slight nod of his head. He must have seen understanding glimmer in my eyes.

"With God nothing shall be impossible,"[14] he said.

Elisabeth had miraculously conceived. According to Jehovah's messenger, I would experience a similar conception. Similar, but not the same. The Spirit of God would father my child. My hand flew to my flat stomach. With fingers buried between the folds of my gray robe, I wondered how it would be possible. Had it already happened?

The man in glistening white garments waited. Did he

expect me to have a return message? My throat constricted again. What could a poor girl say to the King of Glory?

Finally, I found my voice. It sounded stronger than I felt.

"Behold the handmaid of the Lord," I said, bowing my head toward the angel, "be it unto me according to thy word."[15]

When I looked up, the path before me was empty. The house was only a few steps away. My foot throbbed, waking me from my stupor. My smallest three toes had blackened ends. A puddle of thick white liquid slowly soaked into the ground.

Who can I tell about this? I can't tell Joseph. He would never believe such a tale. Who would?

Anna huffed, arms crossed over her chest, when she shuffled down into the small room she shared with Father. Father and I had spent time together in the evenings since before my mother died. He taught me to read, write, and do sums. Some might accuse him of defying tradition (only men need these skills). However, teaching his daughter—who in turn taught her sisters—was a necessity. With all the labor required to keep the farm going, he didn't have energy for the record keeping.

I scanned the largest room in my father's house rather than looking him in the eye. I recalled all the hours of sitting here to eat with my family. I recalled sitting around the fire listening to Father's deep voice teach us the stories from the

Torah. Now, the silence pressed against me like a weight. If I listened closely, I could hear my brothers whispering in their bed behind a hanging goatskin less than twelve spans away.

My father's hand patted my shoulder, and I turned my gaze toward him. Black eyes dwarfed the portion of his face not covered by his mostly gray beard. Heli bar Matthat, my father, concealed a host of emotions behind those dark eyes. I blinked to keep the tears stinging my own eyes from betraying how weak I really felt.

I knelt like a common servant at his feet, my hands clenched together. My heart felt lower than the hardened earth beneath my aching knees. He was sending me away to Elisabeth. I hadn't seen her in seven years. She came to care for Jesse after Mother died giving birth to him. Elisabeth, wife to a priest, had no children of her own and could be spared to spend several months with a widower and his three children until a more permanent caregiver could be found.

"I will arrange for you to travel with a merchant." Father's voice, low and gravelly, revealed what his face did not: disappointment, a hint of despair.

"Abba, I swear I'm telling the truth." I sounded like my youngest brother, Caleb, tattling on Jacob, who was closest to him in age.

Father's warm, calloused finger tilted my chin upward. The waning candlelight reflected off moisture in his eyes.

"I have always known you were special, Mary."

My lips trembled, smiling at his words. The tension gripping my heart loosened, making it easier to breathe. He believed in me. Warmth swelled my heart.

"You must not tell others," he said.

A knot twisted my stomach. Not tell others? But once my condition became evident, they would believe the worst about me. Did Father expect me to bear their judgments silently? Heat flooded my face as if I stood before an open flame.

"They will believe what they want," he said. "It is the nature of people to believe the worst. If you tell them . . ."

I watched his throat wobble beneath his whiskers. My shame would be his shame.

"Abba, no," I said, unable to keep a tear from streaking down my upturned face. "People will speak ill of you. I can't bear it."

"If I can bear their scorn, you can bear it." His harsh tone startled me. "We know the truth. Nothing anyone says will change it."

"But Joseph . . ."

Tears choked me. The thought of seeing pain in his gentle eyes raked across my soul. His opinion of me mattered almost as much as my father's. Joseph was older, but he had pursued me specifically, even though other girls had more appealing dowries. He would know we hadn't been together. He would think I had . . .

More heat flooded through my face and spread down my chest until I thought I might burst into flame.

"We will meet with him together," Father said. "I will explain your situation to him. Just the three of us."

"I'm sorry."

How could calloused hands be so gentle? He pulled me up, holding me on his lap as he often did with the young ones.

I couldn't remember the last time I was held this way. Safe, for the moment, in his arms.

"Never be sorry when Jehovah's plans are not your own." His warm breath, smelling of wine and thyme, tickled my cheek. "His ways are not our ways, daughter. They are higher. We can't understand, but we can obey."

My chin shivered, making answering him difficult. "Yes, Father."

My father's reputation would soon lie in ruins. And it was all my fault. No man would ever marry me. I was sullied. I tried to imagine sharing this house with Father and Anna and the young ones, carrying my own child bound to my chest. Anna would dislike me even more. It would be worse than a death sentence.

And so I sobbed late into the night. Did I even weep this much when my mother died? My pillow muffled the anguished sounds, so my siblings slept undisturbed around me.

I spilled so many tears that night I doubted the straw inside the linen cover would ever be dry again.

A Pondering Heart can be purchased at your favorite retailer.

MEET SHARON HUGHSON

Sharon Hughson is called to share the truth through stories. Her fiction never shies away from difficult circumstances because she wants it to ring true. Her goal is to present relatable characters handling even the ugliest situations in a realistic way that doesn't dishonor Christ. If it encourages the reader, even better.

Sharon dives into books of nearly every genre but writes mostly sweet and Christian romances. Throughout her life, she's sought the escape offered in a well-told tale, but as she's grown older, she appreciates the stories that reinforce her values the most. When she's not writing or reading, Sharon works as a substitute teacher, travels on adventures with her husband of three decades and slaves over three cats in her Oregon home near the Columbia River.

See all her titles at sharonhughson.com. Visit the Newsletter page to get a FREE story and the latest updates about new releases, events and giveaways. To connect with Sharon, join her Facebook Group to be notified about new books.

More from this author

Sweet Grove Romances
Love's Late Arrival
Love's Little Secrets
Love's Latent Refuge (Coming in 2020)

Texas Homecoming
Love's Lingering Doubts
Love's Returning Hope
Love's Emerging Faith
Love's Texas Homecoming Mini-Series

Biblical Fiction
Reflections: A Pondering Heart
Reflections: A Laboring Hand
Reflections: An Adoring Spirit(Coming February 2020)

Or maybe you're still not sure you'll LOVE Sharon's story. You can read a fantasy novella for FREE by clicking here. Even though the title sounds steamy, it's a sweet romance.

FOOTNOTES AND SCRIPTURE REFERENCES

2. MY TWENTY-THIRD SUMMER

1. Wine in this manuscript doesn't necessarily mean a fermented drink. The Greek word used to refer to it can also refer to grape juice and simply means fruit of the vine. However, because of the lack of preservatives, much of the wine consumed during this period was fermented.

3. MY TWENTY-THIRD AUTUMN

1. Sukkot is referred to as the Feast of Booths or Tabernacles in the Bible. It begins five days after Yom Kippur. See more at Judaism 101

4. MY TWENTY-THIRD WINTER

1. Luke 10:40
2. Luke 10:41
3. Luke 10:42

5. MY TWENTY-FOURTH WINTER

1. Passover
2. The Passover meal is called Seder

7. MY TWENTY-FOURTH WINTER

1. John 11:21
2. John 11:22

3. John 11:23
4. John 11:24
5. John 11:25
6. John 11:26
7. John 11:27

8. MY TWENTY-FOURTH WINTER

1. John 11:28
2. John 11:31
3. John 11:32
4. John 11:37

9. MY TWENTY-FOURTH WINTER

1. John 11:39
2. John 11:40
3. John 11:42
4. John 11:43

11. MY TWENTY-FOURTH SPRING

1. John 12:5
2. John 12:8
3. Mark 14:8

12. MY TWENTY-FOURTH SPRING

1. In other places of this story, wine could be fermented drink, because it is Passover, this reference would be to pure fruit of the vine (likely watered down since grape juice can have a strong taste when fresh-pressed).

13. MY TWENTY-FOURTH SPRING

1. Isaiah 53:10
2. Isaiah 53:4
3. Isaiah 53:11
4. Isaiah 53:11

14. MY TWENTY-FOURTH SPRING

1. Matthew 28:6

15. MY TWENTY-FOURTH SPRING

1. The chuppah is the sexual consummation of a marriage contract. Under the Law of Moses, proof of purity was required. Although this seems a strange and embarrassing custom to us, it was the norm for devout Jews during this time period.
2. A traditional Middle Eastern dish made of burghul, minced onions and ground red meat, most likely beef, lamb, or goat. An outside crust encases the spiced meat and spices and is shaped into torpedo's, balls, or patties and is then baked or cooked in broth.

16. MY TWENTY-FIFTH SUMMER

1. Pentecost, also known as the Festival of Weeks. Read more on Judaism 101.

AN EXCERPT FROM A PONDERING HEART

1. i A span is 28.009 cm or roughly 11 inches. This means the cave entrance was slightly more than five feet high.
2. Pesach is the Hebrew word for Passover, a holy day observed the fifteenth day of the first month, Nisan, every year.
3. Luke 1:28

4. Luke 1:28
5. Luke 1:30
6. Luke 1:31
7. Luke 1:32
8. Luke 1:33
9. Luke 1:34
10. Luke 1:35
11. Isaiah 7:14
12. Luke 1:35
13. Luke 1:36
14. Luke 1:37
15. Luke 1:38

www.ingramcontent.com/pod-product-compliance
Lightning Source LLC
Chambersburg PA
CBHW032136170626
46808CB00006B/2259